YOU HA

MW01106644

YOU HAVEN'T CHANGED A BIT

Stories

Astrid Blodgett

THE UNIVERSITY OF ALBERTA PRESS

Published by
The University of Alberta Press
Ring House 2
Edmonton, Alberta, Canada   T6G 2E1
www.uap.ualberta.ca

Copyright © 2013 Astrid Blodgett

First edition, first printing, 2013.
Printed and bound in Canada by
Houghton Boston Printers, Saskatoon,
Saskatchewan.
Copyediting and proofreading by
Rachel Small.

A volume in the Robert Kroetsch series.

LIBRARY AND ARCHIVES CANADA
CATALOGUING IN PUBLICATION
Blodgett, Astrid, 1964–
You haven't changed a bit : stories /
Astrid Blodgett.

(Robert Kroetsch series of Canadian
creative works)
Issued also in electronic formats.
ISBN 978-0-88864-644-6

I. Title.
II. Series: Robert Kroetsch series

PS8603.L63Y68 2013   C813'.6
C2013-901012-2

The University of Alberta Press is
committed to protecting our natural
environment. As part of our efforts,
this book is printed on Enviro Paper: it
contains 100% post-consumer recycled
fibres and is acid- and chlorine-free.

The University of Alberta Press
gratefully acknowledges the support received for its publishing program from
The Canada Council for the Arts. The
University of Alberta Press also gratefully acknowledges the financial support
of the Government of Canada through
the Canada Book Fund (CBF) and the
Government of Alberta through the
Alberta Multimedia Development Fund
(AMDF) for its publishing activities.

Canada   Canada Council   Conseil des Arts
          for the Arts   du Canada

Alberta
Government

for Herb

CONTENTS

❞ DON'T DO A HEADSTAND

If she'd known what was coming, Karen would have spoken up at the start, way back when Jack had moved their summer clothes and the computer and the travel guides out of the spare room in order to make room for Christie. She would have said something right then and there.

Instead she took the news of Christie's visit good-humouredly and even offered to pick up her up at the airport. Jack had shown her a photograph of Christie sunbathing on a beach, and that was enough for Karen to identify her, though Christie didn't look much like the girl in the picture. When Karen found her, Christie was sitting on a grey suitcase, her legs crossed and her body curled inward. Her thin face was mostly hidden under her brown-blonde hair, which hung over her eyes, and her lips were pressed together tightly. She looked no more than twelve, but that couldn't be right, not by the way she held her unlit cigarette with such sureness. Karen watched the hand that held the cigarette, how Christie moved it from side to side, occasionally making sudden, harsh gestures, and had a sudden image of an orchestra in front of Christie—the strings, the winds, the percussion: all of them craning their necks to see, trying to guess when to play. Impossible to tell.

When Christie noticed Karen, she dropped her hand to her lap. Her eyes narrowed and flicked up and down Karen quickly. "You're Uncle Jack's wife," she said, her face half squint, half frown.

"And you're Christie." Karen smiled. "Hello."

"You look different."

"So do you."

"I'm glad we got that taken care of. Anyway." Christie looked past Karen. "Where's Uncle Jack?"

"Proctoring an exam."

"Huh," Christie said. Karen watched her consider this. Then: "So what took you so long? I've been waiting ages."

"Your flight was early, girlfriend. Grab your suitcase. I'm in the fifteen-minute zone out front." Karen tilted her head in the direction of the doors.

She saw it when Christie stood—the puffball of a belly. Karen turned and walked back outside. Christie pulled the strap on her suitcase. The suitcase was plastered with stickers: "Peace!," "Love!," "Portland, OR," a Canadian flag, a teddy bear holding a red balloon. Christie stepped into the revolving doors and lit her cigarette, took a few drags on the way to Karen's blue Accord, then heaved the suitcase into the open hatchback. She flopped into the car with her bead-strewn handbag. Karen sat beside her.

"Hey, this is a non-smoking car."

"You a fascist non-smoker or something?" Christie tossed the butt outside.

Karen blinked, then turned away and started the engine. She tapped out bits of a Bartók allegro on the steering wheel and tried to reconcile the creature on the seat beside her with the sweet, quiet nine-year-old she'd once met. "When'd you start smoking?"

"And don't you start telling me how to look after my baby."

"God forbid," Karen said. She pulled away, past airporters and taxis and family vans.

Christie stared out the side window in silence. Finally she looked at Karen and said, "Is there always snow here in March?"

"Always." Karen chuckled softly.

"I don't find it funny. This is ugly. All that mucky snow. We're driving in muck."

"It grows on you."

"This must be what they call purgatory. Why'd Uncle Jack move out here anyway?"

"Why don't you ask him?"

"How can I? He's not here." Christie paused and then said, "Dad said Uncle Jack would pick me up."

"He's giving an exam."

"So that's what you meant. He a principal now or something?"

"No. A Phys Ed teacher. Like always." Karen pushed two fingers against her forehead.

"Oh. I thought he was a principal at least. Dad says being a teacher is pretty lame." Christie put a hand on her stomach and turned to look out the window again. "Dad says you're still doing that piano thing."

"That what thing?"

"Playing piano for some hick symphony. He says you don't want a real job like everybody else. You just, you know, play little ditties all day."

"Is that what he says?" Karen said. She wanted to say, You're just, you know, a bastard, Otto. But instead she laughed— hard.

"It wasn't a joke, you know."

"No, I guess not. How are your folks anyway?"

"Is this twenty questions or something?"

Karen took a deep breath and focussed on the dotted line on the highway. She started to count backward, in her head, from three hundred and twenty-seven.

"You always hum like this, Karen?" Christie paused and then said, "Oh, right, I suppose I should say *Aunt* Karen."

Karen didn't say anything until she saw the sign for Ellerslie Road.

"Welcome to Edmonton, Christie."

The girl crossed her arms over her chest and clammed up for the next ten minutes. Karen didn't speak until she parked in the stall behind the four-storey walk-up. She'd had enough teenaged students over the years to know when not to say anything. She turned off the engine and said, "This is it."

Christie struggled up the stairs with her suitcase. Karen unlocked the door to the suite, pushed it open, and gestured for Christie to go in. "Here we are," she said.

Christie stood in the doorway. "You guys live in this dive?"

"Oh, knock it off. You have your own room in this dive." She pointed down the hall to the partially open door.

"Thanks. I think." Christie wheeled the suitcase to the first door on the left, walked in, and shoved the door closed.

Karen shook herself all over and glanced at the kitchen clock. Half past three. She poured a gin and tonic and took it outside to the balcony, sat on her peach-coloured yoga mat and turned her face to the sun. *Peck-peck-peck.* There was the annoying magpie, making its persistent staccato on the railing. Karen took a few sips, then sucked back the whole drink. She set the empty glass down, moved into child's pose, and made up a mantra: no, no, no. She wanted to scream, from the tips of her toes.

The door to the apartment opened and Jack walked in. He saw her on the balcony and made his way over to her.

"Jack, thank God you're here." Karen stood and leaned into him. She hooked her finger through a cable of his thick green sweater. She'd knit the sweater when she first met him, when she knew nothing about him and even less about herself. What a time. What a sweater. Oh, how it fit.

"And? Where is she?" Jack stepped back into the kitchen. Karen followed reluctantly.

"You don't want to know. She's a real piece of work."

"Uncle Jack!" Christie skipped down the hall. Jack high-fived her and caught her in a bear hug. She giggled. Karen peered at her, wondering what happened to the girl she had picked up at the airport.

"Here." Jack went to the fridge, cracked open a can of Sprite and handed it to her. He glanced at her belly. "You've got yourself into a pretty mess, young lady," he said in a mock stern voice. He shook a finger at her playfully.

Jack and Christie dodged around each other for a few minutes, he trying to grab her and she trying to escape. Then he stopped and said, "Hey, what do cows do for fun?"

"Cows have fun? I give up," Christie said.

Karen took a step back.

"Listen to moo-sic. Ha-ha, that was for you too, Karen."

"Oh, give me a break," Karen said.

Jack scooted past Karen and raised his hand high. Christie high-fived him.

"You're like puppies," Karen said. "Are you this loud at school, Jack?"

"Yep. Hey, let's go to the park after dinner and throw a few," he said. "You still on the basketball team this year, Christie?"

"I was for a bit."

"Come September you'll be back on."

"I don't think so, Uncle Jack." Christie widened her eyes until they were so huge and round and innocent-looking Karen thought she was going to puke. A little tape started up in her head: *See Jack. See Christie. See Christie walk. See Jack jump. See Jack jump head over heels.* Whoa, stop.

Karen shook the words away and said, "Uncle Jack, Chef, why don't you make dinner? I need to practice." She had to get away, even for a short time. Her fingers wiggled a goodbye and she went to the piano.

It was just an old upright, a "make-do" piano until they could afford the real thing—a baby grand. Karen's music was still on the stand. That morning she had been playing "Allegro barbaro" with its swooping black streaks of notes. Beside it was the Mozart she was playing with the symphony.

Karen was a concert pianist. Only recently she'd realized that every decision she'd made in her life had led to where she was now: performing, teaching, playing just because. She loved it, all of it. Until this evening, there had never been a time when she could not sit down and play with ease. Tonight, her fingers fumbled over the keys. Her thoughts kept going back to last week, when Jack, while brushing his teeth, had dropped the news that Christie was coming for a visit. Jack's brother Otto had booked Christie's flight several days before. Karen was still baffled by Jack's family. Otto barked out orders and Jack said, Yeah, sure, I'm on it. She'd met the family at the wedding: Otto, his tall wife Marita, the daughter who was now at Carleton, the son who was in junior high school, and Christie, who should be in high school. They'd all worn fancy clothes to the wedding, even though Jack and Karen had wanted it to be casual; they made the usual bad jokes about the climate, the downtown architecture, and the "shrubs you prairie people call trees"; they turned their noses up at the food and drank copious amounts of alcohol—and then left. Karen hadn't seen any of them until Christie showed up.

Karen set the Mozart to the side and pulled out a Brahms sonata. After a few minutes she was aware of Jack standing in the archway between the small kitchen and the living room, aware of his patient waiting. She stopped at the next cadence and looked over at him.

"Soup's on!" Jack said.

Karen pulled the lid over the keys and followed him to the table.

Christie, who was already seated, pulled the earplugs out of her iPod. "You play that old people music all day?"

"Hey, be nice. It's her job," Jack said. "She's a pro." He looked at Karen quickly, a hint of an apology flickering across his face, and then looked away. "Omelettes," he said soberly, flopping wedges of folded egg on their plates. "Christie," he said after a few moments of silence, "when your aunt Karen cooks, tell her you like her cooking and you'll be best buddies. It worked for me." He smiled at Karen.

"So," Karen said, looking at the girl, "here you are." In a pretty mess, she wanted to add, but she knew she couldn't pull it off the way Jack had. "You're about to have a baby. Are you going back to school afterward?"

"What?" Christie spluttered through a bite of egg.

"You're still in school, aren't you?"

Christie sent her trapped-doe eyes in Jack's direction.

"Oh Lord, don't tell me we're going to sit around and *not* talk about your baby," Karen said.

Christie dismantled her omelette with one tine of her fork. She put bits of red pepper and green onion into piles on one side of her plate.

"You don't have to decide now," Jack said.

So quick, Karen thought. *See Jack come to the rescue,* her mind tape said.

"What has Otto said?" Karen asked. *Otto who says jump.*

"I don't care what my dad says," Christie said. "It's not his baby. It's my baby. I'll do what I want with it. Stop looking at me like that."

Jack ate heartily but didn't say anything. After a few minutes, Karen looked over at him. "Nice omelettes. Thanks."

Christie shoved her plate away and disappeared down the hall. Jack cleared the table, whistling. Karen filled the sink with water.

"I have a bad feeling about this," Karen said.

"Teenaged girls are like this. Just be patient."

"Fine. But I want it noted that I have a bad feeling."

A few minutes later, Jack tapped on Christie's door and asked, "Coming to the park?"

"Yeah, sure. Soon as I'm done texting."

They had gotten as far into the two-block walk as the end of their street when Christie said, "Oh, I have to go back. Uncle Jack, can I have the keys? Which way are we going? I'll catch up."

Jack set his keys in her palm, nodded in the direction of the park, then took Karen's hand and watched Christie walk away. "She's terrific, isn't she, Karen."

Karen pulled her hand away from Jack and frowned at him. "What planet are you on?" she asked flatly. "No. She's not."

"I wonder what she went back for."

"I don't know. Probably to go to the toilet or to text her friends. Or maybe to get her cigarettes."

"Isn't that bad for the baby?"

"Try to tell her and she'll bite your head off."

Christie came up behind them clutching an unlit cigarette and a lighter. They crossed the street to the park.

"Christie," Jack said. He looked at her cigarette. "I'm worried about the baby."

"Oh, yeah. Right." Christie shoved the cigarette into her pocket.

Wow. See Christie jump. How amazing. How annoying.

"Thanks, pal. Here, catch." Jack ran away from them and

sent the Frisbee back to Christie. "Stay there. Don't run. Don't hurt the baby. I'll keep sending it right to you."

Karen rolled her eyes and walked around patches of dirty snow, watching the two of them. Jack more than Christie. That was Jack all over—silly and fun. But somehow he seemed different.

When the sun disappeared behind a stand of spruces, Jack said, "Let's go back. You don't want to catch anything."

"Give her a break," Karen said. "She's just pregnant, for Pete's sake!"

"I was ready to go anyway, Uncle Jack," Christie said.

When they got back to the apartment, Christie told them she was tired and went to her room.

"The flight probably did her in," Jack said. "And the time difference."

"I'm sure it has nothing to do with all that prancing around with you," Karen said. She sat in bed and leafed through the Alberta Piano Teachers newsletter.

"What's wrong with a little fun?" Jack got in beside her and opened a fat biography across his knees.

Karen tossed the magazine to the side, grabbed his book, and dropped it to the floor. "Hey!" she said as she flopped on top of him.

"Stop, her room is right there," Jack whispered. He pointed at the wall. "She'd hear everything."

"No kidding." Karen sat up and gave him a hard look. "How long is she going to be with us?"

"Till she has the baby. Otto wanted her away from her friends till then. So she doesn't have to explain or be embarrassed or whatever. Then she'll go back."

"You're joking." Karen slid off him.

"Don't be upset. He's my brother. It's complicated. I'm sorry. I'll make it up to you." Jack put his hand on her flat stomach and whispered, "Hey. Maybe it's catching."

"Oh, for Pete's sake." Karen lifted his hand away and set it on his thigh.

Jack sipped his coffee and then bit into his piece of buttered toast. Karen smiled at the minuscule bit of grease by his left dimple. He could never eat toast without leaving that shiny little smear. Some days she imagined licking it off him. Today she took a napkin and wiped—hard. He made a face.

After Jack left for work, Karen telephoned her doctor and made an appointment for Christie. She swept the cigarette butts off the balcony and spread out her yoga mat. Even with the butts gone, the balcony was not the same. It would never be the same. Christie had left her mark with her smoke, her huffs, her angry glares. Lying on her back, her legs straight up in the air, feet flexed, Karen let her mind drift to the first night she and Jack had spent in the apartment. The air had been so hot and heavy they'd unrolled the camping mats on the balcony and sprawled out on them. It was only marginally cooler outside, but a breeze came, once, and it was enough for them to hope for another. The huge elm was in full leaf. Karen was giddy. She was giddy from Jack's silliness, from making love with him for the first time, from trying not to be seen or heard by someone on the street. They were clumsy, and he was done before she really got going. She giggled hysterically, even when he put a hand on her belly and said, "Stay put. Don't do a headstand. Don't do one of those twisted yoga poses." She had thought he was outrageously funny and hadn't stopped laughing even when her eyes teared.

Karen got out of savasana and went inside to the piano. She played through the Mozart first, then the Bartók, and finally some Schumann. She played from memory until she started to relax. Outside, the magpie flew up, landed on the railing with a twig in its beak, and flew off again. Then it was back, mocking her with its maniacal rhythmic pecking.

"Is this all there is?" Christie stood in the archway between the kitchen and the living room and stared at Karen. When Karen didn't stop, Christie said, more loudly, "Is this all there is?"

Still playing, Karen asked, "Is what all there is?"

"Weren't you even listening?"

Karen finished the phrase and stopped. She looked at the girl's baby face. At her fair skin, pug nose, pimply forehead.

"Raisin bran. Is that all there is?" Christie pointed to the table.

"There's bread on the counter. You can make toast."

Christie whispered something.

"Pardon?"

"Fuck. I said fuck. Am I allowed to say that around here?"

Karen got up and closed the piano. She could have sworn the girl had said something else. "I'm off to a rehearsal. I'll see you later."

The conductor studied the music on the stand in front of him. He made small movements with the baton in his right hand and turned pages with his left. Once in a while he looked up and wiped his forehead with his handkerchief and smiled. It was his worried smile. The rehearsal hadn't started yet. The principal violinist was late. The violinists in the back row were still putting in their earplugs. Even with the Plexiglas dividers, they were being blasted from behind by the trombones. The oboist whipped out her reed knife and scraped her reed frenetically, then sat up straight and calmly played her A. The strings joined in, then the winds. At last the conductor lifted his arms, flicked the air twice with his baton, and Karen settled in.

During the break Karen met the bassoonist near the water fountain. "Two rehearsals to go," Colette said. "He's not holding up well."

"He's always like this before the performance," Karen said. She drank, then waited as Colette did the same.

"And?" Colette said. "Sullen?"

"I had no idea."

"Texting in her room? Sleeping till noon? Backtalk like nothing you've ever heard? Attitude?"

"You forgot sucking up to Jack. Calling me a bitch."

Colette's eyes widened. "Oh, that bad."

After the rehearsal, Karen walked home slowly, past Tannenbaum Shoes, Pete's Pianos with the baby grand in the window, Only Organic with its overpriced strawberries and ancient grains, and Cilantro Café. She wanted to call Jack and ask him to meet her at Cilantro. Before Christie arrived, she knew if she called he'd be over in five minutes. Now, he'd want to bring Christie. Not that. Karen stopped and looked in on the diners and reminded herself that in just a few months this time would all be a distant memory.

Jack was in front of the stove when Karen got back to the apartment. He pressed cumin seeds into the palm of his hand and tossed them into a sizzling pan. Christie stood with her back to him at the sink, rinsing broccoli.

"I said bored," Christie said.

"Karen, you're home. Here." Jack handed her a glass of wine. "It's been breathing for quite a while." Karen wrapped her hand around the glass, but he held it just long enough for her to take in his other, unspoken question: What took you so long?

"Christie," Jack said. "There are programs out there. Karen, what programs are there?"

"We'll ask my doctor when I take you in, Christie."

"They'll just tell me what to do and what not to do." Christie tossed bite-sized florets into the steamer. "What to eat. What not to eat. When to go to bed. When to get up. Like it's not even my body. Like it's not even my friggin' baby." She stomped out of the kitchen and slunk down the hall to her room.

"She's killing that baby," Karen said.

"What?"

"She still smokes, you know. Whenever you're not here."

"Karen. I can't fix everything." Jack's face was tight. "I'm just the uncle she can goof around with. Other than that I'm a useless dolt."

"Did you call Otto?"

"Yes." Jack tossed chicken pieces into the pan.

"And?"

"No plans." He lifted a pot lid and backed away from the steam.

"No plans? That doesn't sound like Otto."

Karen had tried to like him at one point, for Jack's sake. But she stopped trying the year Jack set out to make arrangements to fly his mother from Victoria to Edmonton for a visit. Otto caught wind of the plan and said that the cold would kill her; she should really go to Miami instead. Everybody should go, Otto had insisted—Otto and his wife and the three children and Jack and…what was his fiancée's name again? Jack repeated this part of the phone conversation as if it were a joke, shaking his head and chuckling at his hair-brained brother. He stopped when he saw that Karen was not laughing. They might have managed it, financially, but Karen told him she had performance exams and wasn't really a beach vacation person anyway. He didn't question it. She wondered sometimes if that had been the first white lie between them.

Christie came back from her bedroom.

"Karen, I know!" Jack slapped his forehead.

"What?"

"Piano lessons. You could teach Christie."

Christie made a face and shook her head. "I don't think so, Uncle Jack."

"It would be fun. Karen's good, you know. She has a waiting list. For students."

"Uncle Jack, not that kind of music. It's so repetitive and boring and—"

"Come on, just try it. It would be something the two of you could do together. Karen can make it interesting, can't you Karen? You know, find some music she'd like? What do you say?"

"Oh Jack, you heard her, she's not interested."

In their bedroom later Jack said, "Karen, you could have said, 'Yeah, I'd just love to teach her how to play piano, Jack, it would be fun. Whenever she's ready.' Won't you please make an effort here?"

"To what?"

"To like her. It would probably be fun, playing with her. She's going to be with us for a few months still."

"You know it won't be fun."

Jack looked at her. He touched her beside her mouth.

"She's going back, as soon as the baby is born, isn't she, Jack? And someone will adopt the baby?" Karen hated not knowing and she hated having to ask. She put her hand on the green sweater, poked a finger into it, and pulled gently. It was snugger than when she had first given it to him. She ran her fingers over the twisted cables, the baubles, the mini craters. The sweater was for him, but it held both of them; she had thought of the two of them and their life together while she knit it. She had the tension just right. The sweater made her think of how they were connected during the day—him at work in the west end, her at the piano—joined by a taut wire, not too loose, not too tight, just right. Now the wire had Christie hanging from it like an aerialist and doing loop-de-loops. Karen pulled her hand away.

Jack pulled off the sweater and emptied his pockets slowly. He put keys, black wallet, loose change on the dresser. "You, uh, took a while coming home today."

Karen considered what to tell him. She could mention the baby grand, or how she had wanted to call Jack and have him meet her at Cilantro. She could tell him she'd stayed outside the restaurant for a long time, peering in the window looking for a couple like her and Jack, the way they were before Christie arrived. Cilantro was the restaurant where Jack first brought it up, ages ago, before they were married, even. He couldn't wait, he said. It was fine that she wasn't ready—she'd be ready soon. Anyway, she was young, so they had a lot of time. They ordered more wine and loosened up, and the talk escalated over dinner. By the time the champagne mousse arrived—champagne mousse!—they were all hepped up with the details: would they have two or four? Three? One, and travel? Would they leave the downtown and live in the 'burbs? Or on an acreage where they would become eco-friendly and healthy, make their own cheese curds and grow their own sprouts? The more they talked, the more ridiculous it all became. She laughed at all of it. Jack was so good at funny. *He should go on the road with his comedy act,* she thought.

Lovemaking had been fun, too, at least till he started leaving pamphlets on in vitro and adoption on her pillow. Only then did she see the other side of his funniness. There was something disturbing about it—and yet she had helped create it; she had laughed along with him. But all that time, getting her performance degree, building her roster of students, she'd felt like she was sailing higher and higher. When it dawned on her that she could carry on as she was and not have a child after all, it was as if she'd grown wings. Who plans their entire future in one night, she wanted to ask him when he looked at her in a certain way, when it seemed that things had shifted for him somehow. Who? But she would not ask him; she didn't want to hear his answer. Karen had tossed all those pamphlets into the recycling bag without reading them. Jack didn't say anything, but he knew; the pamphlets stopped coming and he stopped talking about where to live and how.

Standing outside Cilantro and looking in at the couples who hung over their glasses of wine like sun-baked sunflowers, she knew that that long-ago silly conversation had been between two other people, between good friends sitting so close that nobody could walk past, and she and Jack had leaned in toward them and eavesdropped shamelessly, and then, when all was said and done, clinked wine glasses and laughed with them.

"The rehearsal ran late," was all Karen said.

"What time's curtain?" Jack asked.

"Three."

"Christie didn't seem too interested when I mentioned it. I thought I'd take her to Fort Edmonton this afternoon."

"Oh." Mimicking him, Karen said, "You could have made more of an effort."

"What does that mean?"

"Nothing. You know, I'm not sure I want her there anyway."

Jack had never missed any of her big performances, except when he had been in Miami with his mother and once when he had been sick. Karen wondered if his absence should mean anything. She tried not to think about it but couldn't help feeling unsettled.

Jack and Christie weren't home when she returned to the apartment after the concert. In the living room, Karen played Brahms, Schubert, Bach. After two hours, they were still not back. She moved the bed under the window—away from the wall between her room and Christie's. She went to the kitchen and foraged through the fridge, poured white wine and nibbled crackers. Then she sat at the piano again and played Mozart, Prokofiev: the sonatas with the fast, swooping black notes. She plucked the keys hard and fast in a crazed mocking of the pesky magpie.

It was dark when Jack and Christie returned. Karen was in bed, flipping through *Orchestra News*. She heard their low, easy voices floating through the open bedroom window from the balcony, too soft for her to make out their words. Every now and again a breeze came up and the elm branches brushed the railing gently. She closed her eyes and imagined Jack and Christie standing side by side, staring at the street below or up at the night sky, and talking the way she and Jack used to, before Christie arrived. She saw him in that green sweater, knit together with all she imagined they might be together, and wanted to find a loose thread and pull and pull and pull.

After a time Jack came into the bedroom and lay next to Karen. There was a small gap between them on the bed.

"She's growing," he said, finally. "Not long now."

Karen lay there for several minutes waiting to feel relief, but none came. She wondered what to say and finally, when she didn't say anything, Jack rolled onto his side, with his back to her. In less than a minute she heard his light snoring.

Nesting was over. Karen almost missed it, but one day she had seen the magpie fledglings, and today she noticed they were gone. The mother bird had come to the railing, tilted its head, and looked at Karen with its hard, beady eyes. *That quick,* she thought. *That easy.*

"I'm going to stay," Christie said. She had been out on the balcony and made the announcement when she stepped inside. She shoved her lighter into her pocket and tipped cereal into a bowl.

"What?" Karen poured the dregs of her coffee down the sink.

"I'm going to stay here. I'll ask Uncle Jack about it. He'll let me stay. With the baby." Christie ate slowly. Her eyes looked small in her round face. Her bathrobe no longer closed around her. "I know he will."

"You might want to ask me, too."

Christie looked surprised.

"What do your parents say about all this?" Karen asked.

"You didn't talk to them, did you?"

"No. You know that it's Jack who talks to your parents." She watched Christie stir her cereal. "But your staying here is not entirely up to Jack."

"We'll find out, won't we?"

See Jack jump.

Karen felt sick during her afternoon rehearsal. When she got home, she glanced at the piano and then turned away. She sat on the couch and shifted four times, then went back to the piano and leafed through the sheet music. Mussorgsky, Schumann, Tchaikovsky. She walked over to the bookshelf and slid her finger along the familiar spines. Nothing there. Her ear ached from the strain of listening for the key in the lock.

And then it came. Karen's feet carried her to the hall in one go. And there was Christie. They stared at each other, then stepped back when Jack pushed the door open.

"Wow," Jack said. "What a welcome. I'm a lucky guy tonight."

"Jack, come and sit down," Karen said.

"I'd love to." Jack laughed.

"Uncle Jack," Christie said.

"Jack, come here," Karen said. Her voice was rising and she didn't know how to pull it down. She imagined it was a loose strand on his sweater. *Just pull,* she thought.

"Let me take my shoes off," he said. His coat was slung over his arm. He set down his gym bag, slipped out of his shoes, hung his coat in the closet by the door.

"Uncle Jack," Christie said again.

"So, uh, what's for dinner?" He looked at Karen uneasily.

"Uncle Jack."

"What's going on?" Jack said. "Something's going on."

"I want to stay here," Christie blurted. "With you. And the baby."

Jack laughed heartily and looked relieved. "Oh, well. That's all."

"Not an option, Jack," Karen said.

A shadow crossed over Jack's eyes.

"Not an option," Karen repeated. She walked down the hall to her room and pulled the door shut firmly after her.

Jack tapped on the door, then walked in and closed the door again.

"Don't be upset," he said. "Give it some time."

"Give it some time?" Karen yelled. "Jack. Tell me she's going home with the baby. Don't tell me again that Otto has no plans. Since when does Otto have no plans? You'd think he's already determined the baby's future. You'd think he's found a nice childless couple for it... Oh, no."

Jack looked at her and didn't say anything.

"Not us."

Jack gave a half nod. It was so quick it might have been a twitch, but she understood.

Karen sat down hard on the bed. "He planned this from the start, didn't he?"

Jack looked away.

"Oh, you. Go away."

"Just give it some thought at least. Think on it. Please," he said quietly.

Karen pushed past Jack, made her way out to the balcony, and leaned over the railing. Her stomach flew up to her throat. It wasn't pre-performance nerves or puking over Jack falling for Christie. Her whole body shook and heaved, but nothing came out. She was empty. She held the railing hard to keep from falling. After several minutes she heard a voice from the far corner.

"I do that all the time," Christie said.

"What?"

"I barf all the time." Christie's belly stuck straight out. "Dry. Nothing comes out. You get used to it. You can get used to anything."

Ben's squinting over at me. He's just asked what I think of
the tomato, anchovy, and artichoke salad illustrating the front
cover of his latest acquisition, *The Glass House Cookbook*. I'm trying to get through the mail. There's always junk in the mail.
Junk, junk, junk.

Here's an example: "You, Krista Martin, are the lucky win-
ner of the Great Western Sweepstakes. Just fill in the form and
answer the following skill-testing question before November
10 *without* mechanical aid."

Or: "Pair of socks, yours free, with the purchase of any one
pair of Nike Air Icarus running shoes." Mail. I want *real mail*.
Here's something, from the Canadian Red Cross. As if they
don't get enough attention in the news—tainted blood scan-
dal, Red Cross apologizes, blah blah blah—now they have to
come right to my mailbox. This is probably a letter reminding
me that I haven't donated for two whole months. They're getting so impatient these days, like they're desperate or something. Once, you could donate your blood and they didn't
want to see you again for three months. Then it was two and
a half. In a few years, they'll be asking for weekly donations.

"Or d'you want sardines on toast?" Ben asks.

"Uh, what?"

"This awesome-looking salad or sardines on toast?" He slides
his fingers through my hair and gives a gentle pull. A trick
disguised as affection when really he wants my attention. "I'm
itching to try something from this book. It's so foodie. I want
to know what foodies eat. D'you think I should wear a tie? I
mean, we could even dress up for this kind of dinner. How
about...Belgian endive with a dill sauce?"

"Ugh. I'd rather have witchetty grubs," I say. He makes a face
and I start to read this letter from the Red Cross, this letter
that's supposed to be a reminder or maybe an invitation to

their annual awards ceremony because I just have to make one more donation and I'll have filled that fifty-thousand-millilitre sack with my blood fifty times. But there's something else in this letter, something I don't think I'm reading, something I don't exactly want to read and am sure I'm not reading, but the letter is real, the scrawl after the "Yours sincerely" is real, not a stamp, and the form on the second page that you have to cut off and return to the Red Cross so they can release information to your doctor in confidence thanks to some ancient bureaucracy—

"Krista, what?" Ben says, and I see that my hand is on his arm now, on his arm to feel him or maybe to keep from falling down. Funny how his arm is always there, right there.

"Listen," I say, my tongue slowing down, "listen..." I try to put on the mock formal voice we both use when we're goofing around, but this time my voice is becoming thicker and thicker, as if I'm speaking through a big dry sponge. "'Although you may be otherwise healthy, we can no longer accept...federal government regulations...please confirm with your doctor at your earliest...'"

Now I'm moving my mouth but no sound is coming out. They take a sample, don't they, Ben, you've done this too. They take a sample and test for things, and even if it's not accurate, what they find, even if the doctor's test you get later says it's not accurate, they give you this thing they call a *zero recall*. Meaning *don't come back*. Whatever it is, it's not true, Ben, it's not true.

Ben's pulling the letter from me with one hand, putting his arm on my shoulder with the other, scanning the letter, hoping the letter will tell him something. His eyes flit back and forth, alert and intent. He's looking at the letter the way he looks at me when he's trying to work out something I did that he doesn't like or understand, like when I accidentally knocked his soapstone whale off the shelf and it broke into three pieces, or like the day, months after the tornado that blitzed through Edmonton and destroyed homes, killed people, when I told him that nothing I had charged on my Visa that day had come through—look, we got all these thing free: my brown sandals and your Eddie Bauer jacket and the lamp in the bedroom—a freak of nature, Ben, a blip, we've escaped scot-free, no charges, no injuries. Or the way he looks at me when he wants to know something and I won't say it, I hold it in as long as I can, wanting and not wanting to tell the longer he looks at me, even when he cups my cheeks and whispers *vixen*. I fall back against the counter, watch his eyes move over the letter the way they move over my face, and I want to speak but no sound comes out.

"What is this," he says. His eyes are reading quickly. "What is this?"

Nothing, I want to say, it's nothing, it's not true, it's not true. It's not true. Let's just ignore it, maybe it will go away. This is what is true: it's Friday the twenty-eighth of October and it's late now, after seven, too late to call anyone who knows anything. It's late because after work we went to buy groceries, crazy on a Friday night, going to Superstore, but everything we do seems to be crazy and spontaneous. Look: you can see Ben and me making our way slow motion up and down the aisles of Stupidstore, slow because we're a duke and duchess for whom eating is not boring necessity but art, slow because the aisles are congested with titanic shopping carts and children hanging off them, one arm or one leg hooked over the side, women with large bulky handbags hanging from their shoulders, and a bird, yes, a bird—a cockatiel—halfway down the cookie aisle sitting on the shoulder of a man with long red hair.

I move outside to the balcony and Ben follows, not closely, but somewhere behind. I hold the railing and look down at the cars, thinking that even though the letter doesn't say it outright, it only means one thing. There is only one reason for zero recall. Tainted blood. When I turn to look at Ben, slowly, Ben who is looking, mesmerized, down at the line of traffic five storeys below making its way eastward along Saskatchewan Drive, purposefully, I know he must be thinking the same thing.

In the cookie aisle there was a man with a cockatiel on his shoulder, remember, Ben? I want to say, and I laugh lightly and the sound cracks the crisp October air. I laugh because I can see the cockatiel in my mind's eye, but it can't possibly be true, and now I see Ben doing things that can't possibly be true. My shoulders are cold now, and Ben's arms are somewhere else. He's holding himself to the railing and looking down at the cars and thinking things I can't hear, can't even imagine—and I thought I knew him. Dry yellow leaves fall from the elm in front of us and bounce gently over my neck and arms. Ben sweeps brown leaves from the balcony with his foot. The children hanging from the cart in the pasta aisle are pulling pasta from the shelves. Cartons of linguini, macaroni, cannelloni, vermicelli, lasagne, tortellini, spaghettini tumble into the titanic cart, filling it for next week and the week after that and the week after that till all the cartons begin to topple to the floor.

"So, when was this?" Ben asks. His voice is coarse and heavy in the dark. We are lying in bed now, where blankets hide my shivering arms and legs and I wonder how I came to be here, how I got from the balcony where I was watching the cars to this darkness where I cannot see him, I can only imagine him and his body, held now so that I cannot reach him or touch him. I can only hear his voice, his question, floating in a little cloud in the space above our heads, and know that his sleepless eyes must be scanning the dark the way they scanned the letter.

When was what? I want to ask. When was what? Do you think I have this thing they are telling me and not telling me I have? When was what? Do you really mean who was he and when did we do it? Is that what you mean?

"Talk to me. We can't go on until you talk to me. When did this happen?" Ben repeats. His voice is softer now and farther away. When I close my eyes I am no longer certain he is here. The air is so cold I can see my breath. I pull two cans of frozen grapefruit juice from the cooler and move on, move our huge and carelessly empty cart past the red-haired man with the cockatiel and the children hanging from their overflowing cart, move toward the photo section for batteries and film. We need batteries for the Walkman and we need a roll of film because tomorrow is Saturday, tomorrow we are going to Elk Island Park to sit by the lake and take sideways photographs of the bison, crooked photographs of the trees, silly photographs of ourselves, all of it upside down and backward. You cannot be serious when you are having so much fun.

Tomorrow is Saturday and we—I could say that, once, with such certainty.

Moonlight streaks across Ben's face. He is still awake. Two in the morning and he is staring straight up at the ceiling, his forehead twisted, his eyes red. I think only of mistakes, of human error, of mechanical error, a blip. *Somebody has blundered*, said someone over and over. On Monday I will telephone, I will pick up the grey telephone and speak with the one who has made this error. I will put things right and Ben will know me again as he did before. I will be able to say again *tomorrow* and *we*, together, in one breath. But I cannot say it yet, not yet, because I am not so sure.

Stacks and stacks of film hang from thin metal hooks next to the counter where a woman is standing, a woman with a large and bulky handbag with green beads and braids dangling from it and from her. When I reach forward she turns, swinging her handbag, and knocks Fuji from my hand and sends the racks of film crashing to the floor. There are Ben and I in slow motion, pushing our massive, nearly empty shopping cart toward the checkout without film, the film abandoned among the racks on the floor beside the kneeling woman. The cockatiel flies and squawks hysterically overhead, filling the air with small grey and orange feathers. And then, inexplicably, something goes wrong. We are pushing the cart back to the freezer aisle. I toss the juice back into the cooler. The profoundly heavy cart only becomes heavier. I return the mangoes to the fruit section and the pastrami to the deli, and the cart gets heavier and heavier. Even when the cart is completely empty, it takes all my strength to move it, and I do, all night, retracing our steps to the film, which we accidentally left behind.

"When was this?" The voice is thick and slow and heavy. Ben sits across the kitchen table from me. His hand is curled around a sea-blue coffee cup I knew the history of once, when those things mattered.

I reach for a cup and discover that I can't feel it. I can't feel the cup or the tabletop or even my skin. I sit up and look at him. I see now that I have misunderstood his question. I thought he was asking *me*.

"Ben," I say, angry now. "When was this?" And wait for his answer. Did we remember the film? What happened to the film, I want to ask, because I can't remember. We were pushing a cart and then we were here. Something went wrong and we forgot it, had to go back for it, what, what?

The telephone screeches suddenly, sending grey and yellow feathers floating in the dead space above it. Ben picks up the receiver and speaks slowly, then listens for a long time to someone who has a good deal to say, and when he hangs up the phone, he looks at me again, looks without his intense, searching eyes, his body lifeless now, and I say at last, slowly at first, then quickly, "There has been an error, somebody has blundered, there has been some mistake," aware, as I speak, of the suddenness of the leaves dropping in front of the window to the street. I pound the table, harder and harder, till finally I feel it, the side of my fist against the smooth wood.

Ben jumps up. He moves away, first to the living room and then back to the kitchen, now the living room again, now the kitchen. He throws his coffee into the sink. His body lurches spasmodically.

Five storeys below cars move past, without hesitation, without uncertainty. Without memory. Ben and I pass each other in the kitchen or the hall or the living room, move slowly through the apartment, not knowing which way to go, not knowing whether to sit or stand. The air is stifled. Our bodies are stunned. When night comes we lie awake again, vigilant. I try to say those little words, *tomorrow we*, those words that mean Ben and me and together and later, those words that were so simple once but now don't make it past my tongue.

Monday, before light arrives, I stand on the balcony, my hands on the railing, my eyes on the street and the valley and Ben's car pulling into the traffic. I know his eyes are fixed on the pavement, his hands have a firm grip on the wheel, and he knows where he is going.

ICE BREAK

We're a long way out on the lake when the ice breaks. It's late, after three, probably; the sun is low in the sky. We've driven past a dozen men squatting over small round holes on their three-legged stools and staring into the blackness. We haven't found our spot yet. We haven't even seen Uncle Rick.

Everywhere I look outside there's the lake and the sky, both the same grey-white, blurred together so you can't see, way out there, what is lake and what is sky; and here and there in the middle distance, men hunched on stools, dark silhouettes; and up close, the dashboard, dark blue, covered in a thin layer of dust except for the handprints I left when Dad turned too quickly off the gravel road onto the lake and I grabbed on, handprints like claws.

Earlier, Dad had asked Mom to come.

Mom had said no. She always said no. She was doing some work, some financial stuff she needed to catch up on. She'd already told him it was late in the season, the ice might not be good; what did Uncle Rick say? Dad told her they knew what they were doing, they'd been doing it for years, they always assessed the risks before they went out. So she didn't talk about the ice anymore.

She just said, "I know how much you love it."

It was after noon. We'd slept in, my sisters and I, and we'd read the coloured comics and done our Saturday-morning chores. Mom looked over at us, Marla, Dawn, Janie, all in a row on the kitchen bench, eating brunch. Tallest to shortest. Oldest to youngest. Each in our own spot.

"Sam," Mom said, "You could take Dawn."

Sometimes they did that, one parent, one child. Every six months, it seemed, we had a family meeting about it, and it worked okay for a week, one or maybe two of us doing something alone with Mom or Dad, and then they would forgot about it till the next family meeting. Or two of us would want to do whatever it was Mom or Dad wanted to do with just one of us. So it never really worked.

Dad looked at me. "You'll have to get ready quick. Uncle Rick and the cousins are probably already there. They won't put up with any dawdling."

Marla finished chewing and took a swig of milk. "No going to Jack's without me." Sometimes Dad took us to Jack's Drive-In for ice cream, if we were good. Marla couldn't come today. She had a babysitting job down the street.

"No one said anything about Jack's," Dad said. "Hurry up, Dawn." Dad got up and went outside. He looked grumpy. Probably we wouldn't stop at Jack's today because he was in a bad mood.

Mom said she'd pack a Thermos of hot chocolate and some cookies.

In the truck, Dad hits my left shoulder hard. It doesn't feel hard, not now anyway. He hits me again and I turn to look at him, slowly. It takes ages to move my head.

Janie and I cleared the table. Marla went to the bathroom to get ready for her babysitting job.

"Janie," I said. I piled the dishes into the sink, ran water into it, and plunged my hands into the sudsy water. "Want to come?"

"Naw, I don't want to."

"Dad'll probably stop at Jack's." I didn't know if he would or not, but it was worth a try.

"Dawn!" Mom poured hot water into a Thermos. "Don't push. She can go if she wants to, but she doesn't have to."

"But you're making me go."

"Not making you." Mom looked out the window. Dad backed the truck out of the garage. "It's a good chance for you two. You don't do much together." She twisted the cap on the Thermos and went downstairs to the laundry room.

"I don't want to go anyway," Janie said.

"I'll give you a dollar."

His face is red and his mouth is moving like he's shouting, but I can't hear anything. I've gone deaf. His eyes are close to my face and bulging.

"I know something you don't know," Marla sang when she appeared from the hallway. Her eyes were dark with eyeliner and mascara, and her hair was done up in a pony.

"What?" Janie and I said. We were still doing the dishes.

Marla smiled in her teasing way and said, "Tell you later."

"No, tell us now!" I said.

We heard Mom on the stairs.

"Remember Mr. and Mrs. Pichowsky down the street?" Marla said in a loud whisper. She went to the back door and put on her boots and coat. "See ya!" she called out. "Bye, Mom."

The screen door slammed behind her.

His lips are fat and his cheeks are rough and stubbly. He didn't shave that morning. He doesn't shave to go ice fishing.

"What?" Janie asked me. But Mom was in the kitchen now and I didn't want to say. Mr. and Mrs. Pichowsky got a divorce last year and moved. We never saw the kids anymore. They stayed with their mom, who moved to Deepest Darkest Mill Woods. Nobody ever went there because it was miles away, and if you did go there you'd just get lost. That was what Dad had said. Marla must have meant that Mom and Dad were going to be like Mr. and Mrs. Pichowsky. Marla was just being cruel. She always did that, said a little bit of something and then left. I wasn't going to tell Janie what Marla meant. It was too mean.

Mom went down the hall to the big bedroom.

"Mr. Pichowsky went away, didn't he?" Janie said. "And Mrs. Pichowsky went somewhere else."

"Mm-hm." Now I had another reason for Janie to come. If Marla was right and Dad was leaving, then for sure Janie should come today. To have one last visit with Dad.

"I'll give you a dollar if you come," I said again.

"A dollar?" Janie made a face. "That's all?"

Dad yanks at my seat belt, and I pull at it. I'm not just deaf, I'm slow and stupid. I can't unclip the buckle. My body is weighing it down. The front wheels have gone through the ice, the truck is tipped forward, and I'm leaning into the seat belt. My fingers are stiff and fat and useless. They could not take a five-dollar bill and fold it in half and half again if they had to. They could not do anything so delicate and so careful.

If I'd stopped to think about it just for a minute, I probably wouldn't have said it. But it just came out: "Okay, five dollars." Five dollars was a lot. But I really wanted her to come. I didn't want to be alone with Dad. He was always grouchier when it was just him and me. He was scary when he got mad. And he never knew what to talk about with me so it was uncomfortable and we both ended up saying all the wrong things. I'd heard them talking once, him and Mom. He said he'd tried to talk to me and I just wasn't receptive; and Mom said he had to get over it—he had to get over the idea that people would be how he imagined them to be. "You can't change people, Sam," Mom had said.

"Really?" Janie said. "Five dollars?"

"You can have my five-dollar bill," I said. It wasn't just any five-dollar bill. I got it when I started babysitting last summer. It had come straight from the bank: it was crisp and smooth and flat, like a page from a brand new book. There was not a single crease on it.

Janie's eyes lit up. "You mean it?"

I nodded. Mom came into the kitchen. I thought she would make Janie change her mind, but she didn't.

"Show me."

All of a sudden, the sound is turned back on. Dad is swearing as loud as he can. The wheels and now the hood are under water.

I went to our bedroom and pulled it out from under my mattress. "Here," I said, walking back down the hall.

Janie took the five-dollar bill and looked at it closely, both sides. I counted. She didn't say anything for at least twenty seconds. "Okay. I'll come."

She laid it on the table, folded it in half once and then again. Then she slipped it into her jeans pocket and bounced around the kitchen, patting her pocket and making little dance steps with her feet and squealing. Then she tilted her chin up a little and smiled so her teeth showed.

Dad opened the screen door and called, "You ready, Dawn?"

Mom looked at him. "Last chance this season, like you said. Have fun!"

"Janie's coming!" I said.

Dad looked from me to Mom.

Mom nodded. "She wants to. Just take them both. I'll get my work done this way."

Dad unclips his seat belt, flings his body onto mine, and rams his shoulder against the door. He's sitting on top of me now, all of him, pinning my legs to the seat. He's so heavy I can hardly breathe. He pushes against the door again and it opens a crack. Ice-cold water seeps in. He moves off me and undoes my seat belt and flings it to the side. The buckle whacks my cheek. He smashes my hip against the door, over and over, pushing me hard against it. The door opens a little more and water gushes in. He stops and takes a huge breath, looks into the back seat, and howls, long and loud.

We piled into the pickup truck, Janie in the little seat in the back and I in the front. Dad backed out of the driveway.

"Looking forward to seeing your cousins?" Dad asked.

"It'll be boring," Janie said.

"Is that what your mother says?" He pulled onto the Yellowhead Highway.

"No, Dad," I said.

"Are we stopping at Jack's on the way back?" Janie asked.

Dad didn't seem to hear. "Man, I hope Rick's still out there. We were pretty slow getting going." He tapped the steering wheel with one hand. He was already annoyed. "Hey, Dawn," he said, turning to look at me. I hated it when he did that, when he turned to look at me and not at the road. I wanted him to watch where he was going. He wiped his forehead, pushed back his hair. "Mom said to ask you about your reading. How's it going?"

For just a moment, I wished Janie wasn't there. I hoped she wouldn't pipe up and say that it had been weeks and I still hadn't finished the book I'd started. Or tell Dad that she was nearly done the Narnia books. I looked out the window at the fields covered here and there with patches of snow. "Fine," I said finally.

Dad's not angry now. He's frightened. Water fills the foot well. It rises over my ankles and up my calves to my knees and then over the seat. We're sitting in water. I'm running out of air.

Dad shoves my shoulder through the gap in the door and out into the lake. He's forcing me out of the truck, but I grab him, first his head, then his shoulders, and hold on as hard as I can. I don't want to go without him.

"You know, I was never good at reading either," Dad said.

"I didn't *say* I wasn't good at reading," I said. I just took longer. I liked other things more.

"Christ. What I mean is, I had to work at it too. Reading isn't everything." He smacked the steering wheel and looked out the window. "I just wanted us to have a good time together, you know?"

"I know, Dad," I said. "It's okay." I felt sorry for him. I didn't know why, but he seemed to get angry all the time. I looked down at my jeans. They were brand new Levis, bought with my own money. I was wearing them for the first time. I had been over the moon when I got them, but now I didn't find them so great.

Dad pulled off the highway and onto a gravel road. It was huge, Lake Wabamun. The sky was grey-white and the lake was grey-white. We were in a gigantic grey-white dome. The sun was low in the sky. Dead grass poked through the patches of snow near the road.

"Look at all those guys! What was your aunt Helen talking about, telling us not to go on the ice so late in the season? She doesn't know what the hell she's talking about! I sure hope she didn't talk Rick out of going. Aunt Helen, your mother, they have no idea."

"Uncle Rick always waits for us, Dad," Janie said quietly.

He squeezes my fingers together so hard I think they'll break, but he keeps squeezing till I let go and then shoves me out into the water.

It's not cold. It's just like nothing. I shut my mouth tight to keep the water out.

Dad dives into the back seat and grabs the buckle on Janie's seatbelt. The inside of the truck is full of water now. Janie's hair is wet and floats around her face. Dad unclips her and pushes against the door. Her face and hands are pushed hard against the window, her hands banging at it, her lips flattened against the glass.

Dad followed the gravel road along the shore for a while and then turned onto the packed-down snow where the others had driven onto the ice. He made such a tight, quick turn I grabbed the dash.

"Knowing my luck, Rick's probably come and gone, we took so long getting here," Dad griped. "I'll just drive around for a bit till I find him. Did you remember the hot chocolate?"

I nodded.

"Mom packed cookies too," Janie said.

"You can have those if you get bored." He stared at the lake. "I'm sorry if you get bored. People are just different, you know? We can't help who we are. It no big deal, eh?"

"Uncle Rick's there, Dad, look," Janie said.

"Where? For Christ's sake, where?" Dad said. He drove forward slowly.

I looked too. We'd passed ten or twelve men, some of them in pairs, hunched over holes. They were dark shapes in the white-grey globe. I couldn't see Uncle Rick either.

"Keep going, Dad, he's out there, I can see him," Janie said. "Past that guy with the dog."

Dad drove on. And then I heard a loud crack, like a gun going off, and the front of the truck tipped forward. It was like those dreams where everything is in slow motion and sounds are muffled and all the people have gone and only you are left. The truck tipped forward, and then the front wheels were in the water.

The men said they helped me out, but nobody did. I got up on my own, when I finally found the hole made by our truck. After Dad pushed me out, I floated up and hit the ice from underneath. Over and over, I kept hitting ice. It took the longest time to find the hole.

I wasn't in the hospital for long. Just overnight. My new jeans had to be cut off. That was the worst part. It seemed like the wrong thing to be sad about, so I didn't tell anyone. My hip was bruised. And my right shoulder and my cheek, where the buckle hit it. The bruises were there for a long time.

The funeral was on Thursday. Janie's face had makeup all over it. She didn't look like Janie. Her lips and cheeks were red, from the makeup. She looked like a baby, with her smooth, soft skin, but she also looked grown-up. Like she was sixteen instead of nine. Her hair was washed and neatly combed. They had even put makeup on Dad. I looked at their chests for the longest time, waiting for them to move up and down.

I asked Marla, when Mom wasn't near, what she had meant about the Pichowskys, and she said she didn't remember saying anything about them. But her face turned bright pink, so I knew she remembered.

Marla said it felt like we were living in a flower shop, with all the potted mums that filled the living room and the kitchen, some green, some purple—dark, glum colours. There were so many we had to put some on the floor. We were in the news, too, the radio and the newspaper and the television even, and Mom said, over and over, at least he was doing something he loved. I wanted her to say the other part, what she had talked to Aunt Helen about—that she was angry with Dad for going, after she and Aunt Helen had told Dad and Uncle Rick it was late in the season and the ice was rotten. She never mentioned that on the news.

I wanted her to say more about Janie, too. I'd seen her in Janie's room, holding a crumpled blue shirt of Janie's up to her chest, then pulling it till it ripped and crying like she was going to break open, right down the middle, like the shirt. Just once she mentioned Janie, to one of the reporters who stayed to ask more questions. She told the reporter that Janie was just a little girl. An adult has a choice, she said, but a child... Then she saw me and Marla lingering in the doorway, as we so often did in the early days after the funeral, lingered near her, and she stopped talking and told the reporter to go. I kept waiting for her to say something, to a reporter or me or Marla, anyone, about getting Janie's clothes back and finding the folded five-dollar bill in her jeans pocket, soaking wet. But she never did.

GETTING THE CAT

Dwight lay in bed staring up at the ceiling and twisting the telephone cord. He'd said "Yes, Mom" three times and was trying to get her off the phone. It was almost seven at night and about time he got up and got dressed before the day was over. If only he'd done the laundry earlier and at least had some clean socks.

"Dwight, are you there?"

"Yes, Mom."

"Your sister's not doing a thing about it. If it doesn't go, the baby will really have troubles."

"I know, Mom, I—"

"You don't know how serious this is."

"I'm on it, Mom. As soon as you stop talking."

That got her off the phone. After she hung up he called his best friend. "Wagner. I'm getting out of here. I'm going to go live in a tent."

Wagner laughed loudly. His laughter was like thunder booming through Dwight's skull. "Not that again," he said. Wagner had a low, gravelly voice that Dwight needed to hear almost every day or else he would feel slightly off. After two days without Wagner's voice, he started to feel shaky, the same sort of shaky he got when he was out of smokes.

"Will you take a cat?" Dwight asked.

"What?"

"A *cat*. Four legs, fur, claws. Meow." Come on, Wagner.

Wagner laughed again. "Sure, whatever, I'll try to find it a home. Bring the old tom over."

Dwight sat up so fast he got a head rush. "Really?" Wow. Just like that, done with the cat. "I'll be right over. I'll just get the cat."

"Hey, slow down, not tonight. I'm just heading over to Druids. You coming?"

"No, I've gotta get the damn cat tonight or else. I'll just get it and leave it in my apartment overnight." *The bathtub will be a good spot. I probably have a can of tuna.* He had to get the cat now. He knew his mother. She'd keep calling till the cat was gone. He batted at the sudden maelstrom of winged creatures swirling around his head chanting, *The cat, Dwight, the kid's allergies, Dwight, don't you know it's serious, Dwight!*

He pulled on his jeans and a crumpled green shirt he found on the floor. There was one pair of clean socks left in his drawer. He never wore them except in times of dire need—they had a highfalutin red, black, and yellow argyle pattern made of bamboo that only a lawyer type would wear. His sister, Sara, had given them to him the year she drew his name in the Christmas gift draw.

Cursing quietly, he slid his arms into his winter coat and bounded down the stairs and out the back of the brownstone. He could be going to the bar, and instead he was going to pick up a goddamn cat nobody wanted—nobody except Sara, who couldn't keep it anyway.

Tiny, hard flakes of snow whipped him when he stepped outside. It had been snowing all day and the lazy landlord hadn't been out to shovel once. Snow came up over the tops of his sneakers, filled in around his ankles, and worked its way down to his toes. He might as well have been barefoot.

The snow brush was in the trunk, under some old newspapers. He swept the windows and hood. By the time he got into the car his fingers were so cold he almost couldn't hold the keys. He jammed the key in the ignition with the palm of his hand, then flattened the gas pedal a few times and tried to start the car. The engine gave a few pathetic whines. He whacked the steering wheel. The car wasn't going anywhere tonight. So much for the cat.

He rooted around in the trunk and on the back seat under old copies of *Vue Weekly* until he found the long orange cord, jammed under the gym bag. Fumbling, his fingers nearly useless, he managed to plug one end of the cord into the car and the other into the little post sticking out of the snow.

Tomorrow he'd get the cat.

He started down the alley, his hands shoved into his coat pockets and his head bent into the driving snow. The wind stung his cheeks. He nearly walked into a car. Its tires spun in the ruts and sprayed a wall of snow up at him. Idiot, revving the engine like that. Then the driver had the nerve to tap his window and point at Dwight and then at the car. Dwight slogged past. As far as he was concerned, he had done his good deed for the day.

A guy stood in the bank machine lobby, a homeless fellow in a blue jacket and knitted green toque staying warm till he got kicked out. Homeless men always made Dwight feel uncomfortable. He blew on his hands, then deposited the cheque from his dad and withdrew some cash. Sixty bucks, that ought to be enough.

Across the street, Druids's green and white lights winked at him, calling him over. They never needed to call twice. He zigzagged through the line of cars crawling along in thick clouds of exhaust, making out the shapes of drivers hunkered down in thick parkas and peering through tiny holes in iced-up windows.

Wagner was at his usual spot at the back, on a bench next to some girl, blondish, youngish, maybe in her twenties, friendly looking. She and Wagner were nearly at the end of their pints.

"Dwight, here, grab a seat, dump the coat, don't sit on Samantha," Wagner called. "What took you so long?"

"Who's she?" Dwight asked, still looking at her.

The girl smiled and tilted her head to one side.

"Friend I wanted you to meet." Wagner raised his arm and beckoned the server over. "Another round, one for our late friend. Dwight's always late," he said to the girl. "We go way back, me and Dwight."

"Oh, for Chrissake," Dwight said. He sat down opposite the girl.

"Dwight's famous."

"Stop it, Wagner," Dwight said. Wagner got on the Dwight brag-wagon whenever he drank.

Wagner ignored him. "For discovering gold. Up north. This man"—he pointed at Dwight—"had a site named after him."

The server arrived with three pints. Dwight picked up his glass and guzzled half of it. Stress made him thirsty.

"Gold?" Samantha said.

"He's having you on," Dwight said. "I was part of these digging crews." No need to tell her how they put you up in a tent—eight sweaty guys in a tent for six weeks, maybe more. "I'm not doing that anymore." He had no intention of telling her they didn't ask him to come back when the season ended. He would have said no anyway. People weirded out on you in those situations. Hallucinated. Heard voices. Went ballistic if you touched their fork by mistake.

"Samantha, this man sitting before you was in the chess club in high school," Wagner said. "He started a sci-fi book club, too."

"Enough already," Dwight barked. That was another life, high school. The situation was, he wouldn't have made it through if not for Wagner making him go to those clubs. He liked chess, though. Nobody expected you to say much.

"He worked on the railway too," Wagner said.

"TMI," Dwight said. "Too much information," he added, for Samantha's benefit. Railway clean-up. Samantha looked too clean to know about that grimy work and the god-awful motels you got put up in.

"Dwight's been around," Wagner went on.

"Wagner, I said enough already," Dwight said before Wagner could bring up the psycho centre. Samantha didn't need to know about that either. Besides, he didn't want to lose it in front of her.

"Samantha's taking classes over at Metro, Dwight," Wagner said, and silently Dwight thanked him for changing the subject.

Dwight looked over at Samantha. She was pretty. Nice hair, he wanted to say, but he didn't want her to think he was coming on too fast so he said, "I did that once."

"Don't you want to ask her what in?" Wagner asked.

"Well, sure," Dwight said. "Give me time." He took a gulp of beer, then nodded at the server and pointed at his glass. "What in?"

"Computers."

"Oh, I have a computer," Dwight said. He'd left it at his ex's and couldn't remember now whether he was giving it to her or had meant to pick it up. He really didn't care what Samantha did with computers, but he liked the way she smiled, the way she laughed easily, the way she basically knew nothing about anything and he could fill her in. Except she kept wanting to know where the gold was.

More drinks came and eventually a plate with fries and wings and celery sticks.

"One place," Dwight said, laughing now because she was listening—she was actually listening—to him, "one place I stayed in had this neon sign outside my window. You know how they always have a letter missing? Well, this one said NO ACANCY, ha-ha, like an ache, you know, but not."

Samantha laughed like she got it.

"Once, I *saw* a sign go out. Remember, Wagner?" Dwight said. He had told his ex about it, but she hadn't gotten it. There was a lot she hadn't gotten.

"Look over there." Wagner nodded at a round-faced man with a shaved head. "Lapsed monk. You think? Check it out."

"What?" Dwight turned to look at the guy. Nothing monkish about him. Just someone with a bald head, maybe an army guy. You could tell by all the tattoos on his shoulders. Dwight didn't like those alpha males. All that anger in those tight muscles. You never knew when they would blow. Wagner, he could be a monk. Nothing rattled him. He made monks look skittish. *So why is Wagner changing the subject? Am I talking too much? Scaring off Samantha?*

A band started to play, and Wagner asked Samantha if she wanted to dance.

"Yeah, with your friend. C'mon, Dwight."

Dwight got up then and concentrated on not stepping on her toes, and when he figured he had that under control, he repeated the name Samantha over in his mind a few times so he wouldn't accidentally blurt out Carol instead. He wondered when he should tell Samantha about having an ex and about cheque day. In the end he decided he didn't have to, ever. Besides, he and Carol hadn't even been married, and you couldn't say he'd been a father to her kids. It was just that they'd lived together off and on for a few years, so she felt like an ex. Not that he'd moved in exactly, unless you count crashing regularly. As far as he was concerned, she was his ex, and having an ex was not the same as never having had anybody. An ex was a bit like a letter X made with a black felt pen, a mark on something you couldn't erase. He would always have an ex.

He wondered if Carol called it cheque day, too. The cheque wasn't much, just a little to help with the kids' clothes and stuff so it wouldn't look like he had been using her all that time they had been together. Mostly it made him feel more joined to her. On cheque day he stayed with Carol and sat beside her on the couch, close if she let him, and talked and remembered how it felt to make love to her, or how he imagined making love to her. His day always seemed to go better after that. He decided that it would just be for a year, him coming by with the cheques, and after that, well, he wasn't going think about it.

"Earth to Dwight," Samantha said. She had stopped dancing and was staring at him.

"Huh?"

"Want to keep dancing, or go back for another beer?"

Dwight stared at her. He wondered if she was older than him or just more mature. He couldn't tell. He needed a bit more time up close to decide. "Keep dancing."

They danced till the band stopped playing, and he never once called her Carol by mistake. Then the bill arrived and Wagner nudged him a little and looked over at Samantha, and Dwight took it to mean he and Wagner were paying for her. He liked that. It meant he had a bond with her already.

"G'night, Dwight," he remembered Samantha saying to him

before he made his way through the blizzard to his apartment, and maybe she had even put her hand on his cheek, too, and left it there for a few seconds, but his cheek was so cold by the time he got home he couldn't be sure. He imagined she did, anyway. There could be no harm in that.

In his bedroom, a red light pulsed slowly at him from the answering machine. It felt like the light was in his head, poking it, hard. He crawled under the sheets and pulled them over his head so he couldn't see the light—it even reflected off the ceiling, for Chrissake.

The phone rang suddenly, forcing him awake. He drifted back to sleep and dreamed it was his old boss calling to offer him a job, an income, something he could use. Before he got to the part where his boss actually spoke, he heard the beep of the answering machine and was awake when his dad's cheerful voice got recorded: "Morning son, it's your father. Give me a call, will you?"

Was his father crazy, calling him in the middle of the night? Dwight slowly felt his feet. They had been blocks of ice a few minutes ago, when he crashed onto the bed. Out front someone was spinning tires in the snow. Give it up, Dwight wanted to shout. Then he opened one eye and saw his clock radio: it was eight-fifteen in the morning. He reached out and hit the "play" button and let the answering machine fire the messages at him: "Dwight, it's Sara. I hear you found a home for Ralph. Sounds good, but where is it? What's the person like? Call me." And Carol: "Just touching base. I'll try later." And then the message his father had left: "Morning son, it's your father. Give me a call, will you?"

This was hell. Dwight turned on the bedside light and stared up at the ceiling, at the random bits of glass. There was the Big Dipper, almost. It was askew. He liked that it was slightly off—anything slightly off made the world more interesting. Not that it was useful, looking at the world this way. It didn't help him become one of those guys who studies stars for a living.

Dwight stood under the shower for a few minutes. He was

waiting for it to come to him, the thing he was supposed to do today, right off the bat. But what? When he finally went back to his bedroom he saw the answering machine light flashing at him again. *Not more messages.* He felt a stabbing pain in his head.

When he hit "play," he heard Samantha's voice. It slid over his skin like a gentle massage.

So. She likes me.

He replayed her message. She was not asking him to do anything except give her a call, and he had been planning to do that anyway, as soon as he found her phone number. She'd given it to him, last night, at the bar, when they were dancing, probably. He could feel her fingers sliding in somewhere but couldn't picture what she had written on. He squeezed a few shirt pockets, checked his jeans for his cigarette packet. Nothing. His body grew tight again. *Don't lose it, Dwight.* The tiny creatures were circling his head again: *You're losing it, Dwight! You're losing it!* What he needed was a long, long run. That was what Carol had gotten him into, running and eating vegetables, but he knew he'd have a heart attack if he ran half a block.

Dwight wrinkled his nose and shook the argyle socks a little before pulling them on, then found his jeans and shirt. It was still with him, that feeling that there was something he needed to do today, first thing. Something critical. He sat on his bed, stared around the room, and slowly filled up with the familiar, heavy despair that came with not knowing what he was supposed to do or where he was meant to be.

Cheque day, that was it. Cheque day. He would go to Carol's. He'd take her the cheque.

He grabbed his jacket and went out the back. It had stopped snowing sometime in the night and the sky was clear now, still a little dark but clear, and the air was cold. He brushed off the car again and unplugged it. The car gagged and whined and finally started up reluctantly.

A few minutes later he pulled up in front of Carol's condo. He tossed his bulky coat onto the passenger seat and left the

Saturn running in case it wouldn't start again, ran up the steps to her door and turned the handle. The door wasn't locked. He walked in.

Carol flew past him, chasing Jody down the hall, and Steph shouted something from the toilet seat through the open bathroom door. Abby, who was the oldest, fourteen maybe and pimply all over, walked up to him from the living room and made a face. "What do *you* want?"

"What do *I* want?" he repeated. Stalling. He couldn't explain it, how he just wanted to be here.

Carol came back. "Dwight! You got my message." She gave him a strange look. "Where's your coat?"

"Why, you need a coat?"

"It's twenty-five below out there! Aren't you cold?" Carol threw him an exasperated look and reached into his shirt pocket.

He wanted to be here still, at the kitchen table, or shaving in the bathroom; he wanted to be part of this morning chaos, this intense, focussed energy radiating from Carol. He never felt lost or confused around her.

"Oh, good. I'm all out." She pulled the packet of cigarettes out of his pocket. *So that's where I left them.* She took out a cigarette and pushed the pack closed, then looked at him and opened the pack again. "Sa-man-tha." She stretched out the name teasingly. "Look at the fancy way she writes her name, all loop-de-loopy. Cute!" She smiled while she slowly made the shape of each letter with her lips. "Girlfriend?" She pushed the cigarettes back into his pocket, and when she patted them in place he felt like he was a kid being patted on the head. Then she picked up a lighter from the kitchen table and narrowed her eyes when she looked at him. "You gonna call her?"

He felt like a tired mouse running after a dusty cotton ball. Maybe she wanted to know, but maybe she was just playing with him. "I'm leaving. The car's running." He didn't like that feeling, not knowing. "Isn't it time for the girls to go to school?" He was surprised how quiet his voice was.

Carol looked over at the girls. "Off you go, girls. You'll be late for school."

They stood in a row, giggling. If only they would go so he and Carol could be on their own. Just for a minute.

"Go on," Carol said. She tilted her head toward the door.

Abby gave Steph, the youngest, a nudge.

"Did you buy us anything?" Steph asked.

"No." Dwight felt like a jerk. Why hadn't he thought to bring them something, a Mars bar, gum? He watched Steph wistfully. He didn't mind her. Kids were fine till they were eleven or twelve.

"Beast," said Jody, the middle one, and they all repeated it and giggled. They crowded into the entrance and shoved him to the side as they got themselves ready for an expedition to the far north with their moon boots and hulking coats and puffy mitts. "Beast, beast!" they shouted. Then they went outside and pulled the door closed.

"You going to call her?" Carol asked again.

"I brought the cheque," Dwight said. His voice was pinched, like he was being strangled. His mother, his father, his sister, now Carol even, they were all squeezing him, choking him.

Carol shook her head sadly. "Oh, Dwight, I don't need your dad's fifty bucks."

"It's not…" Dwight pressed his lips together and clenched his hands into fists.

"Are you okay?" Carol asked.

"I'm fine." He hadn't mean it to come out like that, through his teeth, but it had, and he couldn't take it back. What does she mean anyway, am I okay? She better not start that.

"I mean it. Are you okay?"

He felt like he was back in that psycho place and she was sussing him out. At first, he hadn't minded. She was the only one who understood where he was coming from. Right off the bat he had told her he was there by mistake. Some mix-up that was too complicated to fix. That's what she had figured, too. And you could see he wasn't like the others. They were all spaced out and bored out of their minds. But soon he was

hanging out with them on the couches or sitting around the
kitchen table with those twenty-cent forks and spoons that
came from Value Village and flicking popcorn kernels at each
other or bending the cutlery into free art. One day it dawned
on him that he was invisible. He blended right into the brown-
and-white sofa or the three guys hunched at the table—he
could be any one of the guys. It wasn't that they all moved the
same way and talked the same way after living together. It was
because nobody did anything and nobody owned anything.
Everything in that house had been left behind, the books and
the records and even the clothes. People came and went and
left shirts and pants that had come from the Goodwill or the
Sally Ann. You weren't yourself anymore; you were a mix of
nobodies. That was the worst. Being that weird mix and not
knowing who you were anymore. Dwight hated that. He hated that even more than he hated knowing he could be bent
up as easily as a cheap spoon or fork, just by the way someone
looked at him or by something someone said.

Carol said, "It's been a year anyway."

"What?"

"It's been a year," she repeated. "That's your last." She gave
him a look that said, It's obvious—why don't you know this?
"Your last cheque," she said slowly, as if he were thick. He wanted to hear something in her voice, regret maybe. Then she
sighed heavily. "You know I don't cash those cheques." She
looked at him with curiosity. "Don't you?"

"Don't piss around with me, Carol."

"Whatever. I have to get ready for work." She walked up
the stairs.

A whole year already? Is she funning me?

"Just leave!" she called from upstairs.

She'd never done this before. He didn't know how long
to wait.

After a few minutes she came to the top of the stairs. He
looked closely, to see if her eyes were red, to see if she'd been
crying, but it was too dark up there to tell. "Just go." She went
back to her bedroom and slammed the door hard.

Dwight pulled his chequebook from his jeans pocket but then changed his mind and went outside. *Fuck her. Not cashing my cheques, all this time? Who does she think she is?*

There was the Saturn, choking and puking and spitting out big grey puffs of exhaust. His head throbbed. He sat in the car and wondered what he was forgetting. Maybe to call Samantha. He could do that, now that he knew where her number was.

He drove forward. Carol wasn't cashing his cheques. How could he not have known that? His brain was totally fried. Maybe it had started last night. He tried to remember what he had done. He'd had beer, maybe a couple beer, with Wagner and the girl, he'd even danced with her, danced till the band stopped, and she'd called him, and now he couldn't remember the way she looked or even how she felt.

His stomach growled. It was a cavernous pit. He pulled out his wallet at the four-way stop. Empty. All that cash, gone. *Sara, she'll give me breakfast, she'll give me a bite to eat.* She was always telling him to pop in sometime. It wasn't far, maybe ten minutes. He had just enough gas to get there.

A plough crawled along ahead of him and piled the snow in a windrow four feet high beside him. The side streets were nearly impassable, with windrows and hard-packed blown snow and cars that had just pulled over and stopped wherever they could—some of them stuck, half-buried in snow, the front or back ends sticking into the street. He drove through deep ruts, scraping the underbelly of the car, and pulled to a stop in front of a blue one-and-a-half-storey. No one had been out to shovel the walks yet. He could do that for them. He could shovel their walk. As soon as he got some food in him.

The front curtains were drawn and a light was on in the upstairs window. Jeff would be getting ready for work or shaving or telling the kids a funny story maybe. No, he'd be gone already. He was a doer, that Jeff. Sara would be serving breakfast. *Holy, am I hungry. Starving.* Sara'd make bacon and eggs and toast, put on another pot of coffee, and they'd shoot the breeze for a while, the way it should have been with him and Carol.

He hopped up the steps to the front door and rang the bell. Through the narrow pane of glass he saw Stacey run up to the door, grinning and waving her arms wildly and running in small circles. Dwight stomped his feet and shivered and wondered how old kids were before they learned how to open doors. Stacey was three or four. Maybe by age five they figured it out.

Finally Sara appeared with the baby boy in her arms and pulled the door open.

"Dwight!" She looked surprised. "Come in."

Dwight looked past her into the kitchen at the other end of the house and there was Jeff, sweeping something off the floor. Chunks of toast maybe.

"We're just heading out. We're on our way to the doctor's," Sara said.

"You guys already eaten?" Dwight asked.

"Eaten? Ages ago. We have to go. If you're here about Ralph...I don't know why Mom had to bring you into this."

Dwight's stomach was giving him pain and his head throbbed. "What?"

"Who is this person who wants Ralph?" Sara asked.

Then he remembered Wagner telling him he had a friend who wanted a cat. "Why does Ralph care?"

"He can't live just anywhere."

"I'm here now," he said. "I found a place." His voice was far away and he had to shout to hear himself. "I'm not coming back. I took my life in my hands getting here today. Could you just get him?"

Sara took a step back and put her hand over the baby's fat, drooling face. "He's a family cat. He needs a family. Is it a family? Do they understand about Ralph?"

"Just give me the damn cat!" Dwight shouted. Didn't she hear anything he said? He had come for the cat. He was doing what she wanted. He was doing what his mother and father wanted. He had it all arranged with Wagner. If he didn't get the cat now, he was done. Forever the loser.

Stacey spotted the cat and ran after it.

"That's right, Stacey, get the cat for Uncle Dwight."

"Run, Ralph, run!" Stacey screamed as she chased the cat up the stairs.

"Christ, I can't believe this," Dwight said.

The baby's face turned dark red and crinkly and he began to bawl.

"Dwight, we can't just give you the cat like this," Sara said. "I don't even know where the cat carrier is. And he'll die of cold out there."

Dwight could throttle her. *Why doesn't she stop the kid?* She just stood there, saying things to him, but he didn't care to listen anymore. He just wanted the damn cat and he was going to get it. He was going to be one of those people who did what he set out to do. He ran after Stacey. Heavy steps came up after him. Jeff's. Now Jeff was shouting. Stacey was crying. The baby screeched like a howler monkey.

Forget the cat. Now all he wanted was to get away. He ran through the nearest door, slammed it hard and turned the lock.

He'd escaped, and they were on the other side of the door, but it happened anyway: his head blew apart. Little pieces of Sara and Jeff and the screaming kids flew out of his head. A shout came from the lampshade on the ceiling, another from the back of the bedroom closet. He heard knocking on the door, then through the window, now from the little bathroom off the bedroom—knocking, pounding, bashing. The baby wailed and Stacey howled. Sara and Jeff hollered at him and their voices were everywhere, screaming, yelling, bawling *Dwight!* and *Ralph!* The words flew around the ceiling and into the bathroom and under the bed. Now the words were flashing above him like those signs outside motel windows with their missing letters: GO! RUN, DWIGHT! CALL RALPH!

He got down on all fours and onto his belly and worked his way under the bed. He put his hands over his ears. It was dark here, and quiet. He was safe.

An arrow pierced his cheek, drawing blood. He yelled. Then he saw it. A claw. Jeff and Sara had a beast in their house, part devil, part wild animal. It hissed and snarled and spat. When

Dwight grabbed it, it shrieked like the baby howler monkey and drove its teeth into the flesh of Dwight's hand, near the thumb. It hurt like hell. The pain shot through his hand, up his arm to his face, and even down to his toes. With his other hand he grabbed the beast by the neck and squeezed. He squeezed the thin veins and tiny bones as he stared into the shiny devil eyes. He squeezed with all his strength until he heard it say *Don't do it, Dwight.* The devil spoke like Wagner, in a deep, gravelly, soothing voice. Wagner. Right here, watching. When Dwight heard his voice, he let go, and the devil darted away, snarling and spitting.

The shouting, the banging, the howling had stopped. He was inside a tomb. He backed out from under the bed and sat against it and stared down at the blood pooling in his hand. His head stopped exploding. All the pieces slid gently back into place. He stared at his blood, his thick, warm, oozing blood. He could feel Wagner still. And at last, he was like Wagner. Calm. So calm he made monks look jittery.

Sara's voice came to him, softly, sweetly, like an angel: "Dwight?"

Then, Jeff: "Open the damn door before I break it down!"

Dwight strolled into the little bathroom and ran cold water over his bleeding hand. So much blood, so much rich, healthy-looking blood. His own. Wow.

He walked to the bedroom door and opened it. Finally, he had a plan and he would share it with Sara and Jeff. He no longer wanted the cat. It was their damn cat, and they could do what they wanted with it. That was the plan. He would tell them. When he stepped out into the hall, Ralph shot through his legs and bounded down the stairs, and Jeff and Sara and Stacey turned and ran after it like Dwight wasn't even there.

❧ LET'S GO STRAIGHT
TO THE LAKE

Here's Connie at last, hours late. Look at her, though. She doesn't look anything like Connie. She's so big she fills the seat and the air around it. But I know it's her. She stares straight at me, her right hand on the steering wheel and her left arm slung over the frame of the open window. So laid back and cool in the driver's seat.

"Meghan!" she calls.

"What took you so long?" I yell. I'm on the bench outside the truck stop café, where the Greyhound dropped me off. There was no way I was going in, not with all those truckers who kept gawking at my chest. "The bus dropped me off an hour ago." My skin is on fire. If we don't go straight to the lake, I'll die. I shove the book into my duffle bag and stand up.

Connie gets out of the car and shouts, "Hey, fish-mouth!" She's a head taller than me, and her hair is streaked with blue. "Close your maw!" She grabs me and hugs so hard she knocks the wind out of me, then bursts out laughing. It's a deep laugh, like a guy's. "You made it! I knew you'd come. And you haven't changed a bit."

Speak for yourself, I want to say. She opens the back door and tosses my bag onto the flattened McDonald's bags and empty cigarette packages strewn across the back seat. I make for the front passenger door. My T-shirt sticks to my back. "I'm roasting. Let's get out of here. Let's go straight to the lake." The lake is ginormous, Connie had told me on the phone. You can't see across it. You think you're at the ocean. An ocean, in Alberta. She sounded just the same, on the phone. It was freaky. After five years. "Let's go right now," I say. "I packed my bathing suit and towel, like you said. Please, let's—"

When I get in I almost squash the tiny kid on the seat but she scooches out of the way just in time. Good grief, not a kid. Connie must be looking after her for the afternoon. The kid better be gone by tonight so we can have our girls' night.

"What do I do with her?" I ask. The girl giggles.

"Just take her on your lap."

The kid climbs right onto me. She's long and skinny and warm and as light as a rag doll. She sucks her thumb, hard, and twirls a strand of my hair at the same time. "Whose kid? Doesn't she have a car seat?"

"Holy hot potatoes, girl, we're not in the big city anymore! There's not enough traffic in Slave Lake for all that. Just hold her on your lap already." Connie guns it down the highway. "Meet my daughter. Amber Joy. She's coming up to two."

Holy hot potatoes is right. I want the car seat to swallow me whole. "What?"

"Yeah," Connie says.

"You didn't tell me."

"Wanted to surprise you. It worked."

Sweat shoots across my thighs like a sudden rash. I wish Janice had come. It was supposed to be the two of us all along, but she didn't show up for the bus.

Connie lights a cigarette. "Sorry about the wedding, eh. All the wrong people got invited. All the right people didn't."

"You got married? When?"

"Ha, got you again. This is what you missed: my mother didn't come, my brother didn't come, and then it was bloody freezing and the church furnace was busted!" Connie turns off the highway onto the wide and sleepy main street. "Holy shit was the priest pissed. He was the first to get tanked at the party after, no surprise there. Well." She puts her cigarette to her lips and frowns. "You get what you pay for."

"So? Did you go to Hawaii? Everybody goes to Hawaii."

"Who goes to Hawaii? We went home!" She stops in front of a yellow bungalow with a covered porch. "Here's home," she says.

I hoist myself out of the car with Amber's legs hooked around my waist like she's a Gumby toy. She clings to me and giggles when I haul my duffle bag from the back seat. Connie pulls a six-pack of Molson and a carton of Coke from the trunk.

"This is why I was late," she says, surprisingly well, through the cigarette jiggling between her lips. She kicks open the screen door to the porch with her sandal. "Watch the kittens."

First I hear the mewling, then comes the whiff of stale cat pee. An orange-and-white striped kitten bounds out of the heaps of shoes and empty beer cans, lunges at my ankle, and grabs hold with all four paws. A second kitten, all grey, bats Stripey's ear, and they tumble away.

"Don't let them in," Connie says. She leans against the house door to open it and walks in. Amber slides down and pats Mr. Grey's head. I cover my nose and follow Connie into the house.

Age thirteen. We're hunters. Sing, "You ain't nothin' but a hound dog," the little bits we know, and dash through her house opening closet doors and cupboards. Sniff out the cigarettes stashed in her mother's sock drawer or in the pocket of a certain longish light blue knitted sweater. Stuff is there for one reason: to be hunted down and swiped. Connie's bedroom is a little girl's: frilly trim above the window, flowery bed skirt, knick-knacks on the bookshelf, and two whole rows of Nancy Drew books, in order by number. We flop on the double bed. Connie's long and skinny and takes up almost no space. She blends into the bedspread. She leans over and pulls a book off the shelf. Behind it is a pack of cigarettes. We tear open the wrapping with our teeth.

"House isn't big, but it's big enough!" Connie calls out. She's already in the kitchen at the back of the house.

"Wow, Connie, your own place."

It's too weird. Janice and I have changed. We're older. I thought Connie would be different too, but she's the very same, except that she looks a lot different and she has a baby. She's not like any mom I know—she's like a kid who never grew up. She's still got her knick-knacks, on top of a little bookshelf full of videos. A huge television set takes up most of one wall. There's a little plastic table and chair. A huge velvet

picture of a lion, above the couch. A brown-and-white plastic
clock in the shape of an owl. It's as if this is her mom's house
and her mom is out, the way it always was.

"Just toss your bag beside the couch, girl." Connie turns on
the floor fan, and it blows warm air at me. I step out of the
way. "It's a Hide-A-Bed. That's where you'll sleep. You're our
first overnighter."

"Hey, thanks." I sit down. The couch scratches my legs.
"When are we going—"

"Meg! Check out the brand-new TV and VCR. Rod just
bought them. He loves watching videos. When he's home
and you can't find him, just check out the couch!" Connie
laughs, not like a guy this time, but in an edgy way. "Hey, Meg,
we can watch movies all night if we want, like we used to!"
She gives a loud whoop. "So, anyway, we're renting. We've got
the main floor. Some guy lives downstairs, oil-patch worker. I
guess Janice called you today."

"No, she call you?"

"Yeah, she's got the flu or something."

"Huh. I wish she'd called me."

Connie had phoned in May. One month to go and high
school was over; why don't Janice and I go up for a night, first
weekend in July? What the heck, Janice had said, let's have a
party, see how the old girl is. I said I'd go if she did. I took my
seat on the bus figuring she'd come flying in at the last minute,
and next thing I knew the bus was leaving without her.

On the TV set is a small picture of Connie and the guy who
must be Rod. The picture is grainy and out of focus. Connie
is about eight months pregnant and large all over. Smiling
her huge smile. Her hair is curled into tight ringlets. She's
wearing a lacy white dress and holding red carnations. Rod
stands beside her, straight and stiff as a Popsicle stick, and
smiles a lopsided smile. He's shorter than her, and thin, but
he's all muscle. His hair flops on his shoulders. The Connie in
the picture looks straight at me, hard, like she's saying, "Look.
C'mon, have a good, long look." Rod stares somewhere over
my shoulder.

Connie turns the photograph facedown. "Oh. Don't look at that. You going to university come September, you and Janice?"

"Yeah, you too?"

"What, I'll take Amber with me?"

"Yeah. Right." I keep forgetting about her kid. "I'm taking—"

"Not for me, I decided way back, before Amber. University kids, they're so smart they're stupid, brains but no sense, know what I mean?"

"Yeah, I know what you mean." I say it slowly. I'm trying to figure out if she means me along with all the other university kids. Amber scooches toward me on her bottom, scissoring her legs up and down at lightning speed. I take her on my lap. She's warm and wet. Her diaper sags halfway down her legs. "Eww." I plunk her beside me on the couch.

"She can talk, but she doesn't like to." Connie stares off at something out the window, at a tree or the sky for all I can tell. She runs her fingers through her hair. "Same with walking. The public health nurse said it has to do with Rod being away a lot for work." She sounds bored. Like she's talking about someone else, not her own kid. "Him coming and going and no routine and his way."

Amber reaches over and hugs me again.

"She's not an animal. I don't want her climbing all over you," Connie says angrily. "Amber, go sit in your chair for a while."

In no time Amber's off the couch and back on her plastic chair. She watches me and flicks her earlobes with the tips of her fingers.

"It was just a hug," I say. The heat is suffocating. I want to be outside. I want to be in that ginormous lake.

"What do you know about kids?" Connie says back.

Janice would know how to laugh it all off and get us back on track. I can't think of anything funny to say. "I teach swimming. To kids." It sounds so lame I wish I hadn't said it.

"Don't you be like those public health people, acting like you know what I should do with my own kid. I know what I'm doing. I'm keeping her in line so I don't have problems later. My mom warned me, keep her in line." Connie drops her cigarette butt into the white bowl she's holding and puts the bowl on the coffee table. "Not that she gives a damn about Amber." She gets up and takes Amber's hand. "Let's go change you."

Age fourteen. Connie's mother isn't home. Again. Working, maybe. Maybe not. We go up to Connie's bedroom, Janice and I, and watch movies on Connie's television and giggle hysterically. Then we play cards, for nickels. Janice and I don't know any card games except for war and crazy eights. Connie teaches us grown-up games like crib and rummy and 21.

Connie comes back with Amber. She takes hold of Amber's shoulders and points her toward the plastic chair, then flops onto the couch beside me.

"We were in a cabin in the bush, Rod and me, a log cabin, till we got this place. No running water, no power, nothing. And then Rod got on with a logging crew. I was working at the pet store in town till I had her. You seen those tarantula spiders everybody wants?" She doesn't wait for an answer but just keeps talking. She talks so fast I feel like she's sent a ball spinning around my head, faster and faster. "I wanted one, but he wouldn't go for it. He never goes for what I want but oh well. The kittens we got from a neighbour when they were weaned, four of them, but two didn't make it. They were too young to be away from their mother." She hasn't let out a breath yet. She keeps inhaling. "We moved in last fall and put in our daffodils and tulips right away, plastic ones so we have flowers all year." She'll explode if she doesn't let out some air. "Everybody around here does. I love it! Ha!"

I burst out laughing and realize I've been holding my breath, too. "You're so funny, Connie."

Amber shrieks. It's a happy sound, but it's so high both Connie and I wince.

Connie stands up quickly and says, "Let's go to the 7-Eleven, like we used to."

"Sure," I say. Anything to get outside.

"Don't you remember, Meg, every day after school. Only it was the Red Rooster, or the mall. You'd get an Aero bar, I'd get a Cuban Lunch. Then we'd go home and play backgammon or crib. I whipped the pants off you. You weren't good at games, were you?"

Connie's got it wrong. She's got it all wrong. Janice and I never told her, though.

Age twelve. Grade seven, new school, no friends. Except Connie. Nobody wants to play with Connie. I play with her and I let her win because I think she won't play with me if I win. I never tell my parents where I am, but they know. I come home and my mother says, *I can smell that cigarette smoke on your clothes and in your hair. I can smell it as soon as you walk in the door.* I wait for her to say I can't go over anymore, but she never does.

I move quickly through the pee stench and wait on the bottom step while Connie pulls the stroller out from behind the garbage bags. "Hey, Connie, can we go to the lake when we get back?"

"This thing is such a piece of crap," Connie calls.

I have a bad feeling about the lake. Earlier I wasn't sure, but now I know Connie's ignoring me whenever I mention it. She yanks the stroller open, yanks and yanks till something finally gives. Then she holds it above her knees and walks down the steps. "Come on, Amber. Hop in. Hands on lap."

Amber climbs into the stroller and starts to flick her ears with her thin fingers. Connie doesn't see. She points at a brown house and tells me about the family who lives there and how loud the fights are whenever the old man gets home. "You can hear glass breaking," Connie says. "And wood crunching. Maybe he's throwing the furniture. I'd love to be a fly on that wall." At the next house is a woman who sometimes takes care of Amber when Connie and Rod go to the bar.

Connie's chatter is like a piece of plywood slowly bearing down on me. My head feels puffy. Sweat seeps out of my armpits, behind my knees, out of my scalp, around my eyeballs. I can't stop thinking about the lake. Let's go, let's just plunge in with all our clothes on.

The air conditioning in the 7-Eleven chugs loudly. It's a

freezer in here. I don't want to leave. I silently will Connie to take her time.

We go straight to the chocolate bar aisle.

Age fourteen. It can't be Smarties; they rattle. It can't be anything long, like a Mr. Big bar. It can't crinkle too much. Licorice crinkles. Something small. A peppermint patty. Cuban Lunch, maybe. In the right pocket, in the right way. A block past the store we tear open the chocolate bars and eat quickly. We drop the wrappers on the sidewalk and pretend not to see them.

Connie walks on and grabs a box of Popsicles. Then she comes up beside me and picks out a Mars bar. "You getting one too? Aero bar? They don't have mint anymore, but…"

I look at Connie, catch her eyes even, but they don't tell me anything. When I shake my head, no, a shadow crosses over her face. It's like I've let her down in some huge way. Connie takes Amber to pay and goes outside to wait for me.

I wish there was something I wanted. I bask in the cool, then step outside.

"Here." Connie holds the box of Popsicles toward me. I take one, grape. It's already melting. Juice drips under my chin and along my arms to my elbow. Amber starts to giggle, and she's so cute I giggle along with her. Even Connie starts to laugh. We linger in the shade of a large elm, then dash across the baking sidewalk to the next piece of shade, hunch under the branches, and dash again, all the way to her house. Laughing. Amber shrieks so hard she has a coughing fit.

At Connie's house, we sit on the front steps for a few minutes, but it's so hot in the blazing sun we go inside. Connie doles out more Popsicles and we sit on the couch and lick. My arms and legs are purple and sticky. I feel grubby all over. Connie talks on, loudly and endlessly. My head hurts from the blast of words and the zigs and zags and U-turns. I feel a bit sick. I know it for sure, and knowing makes me feel sicker: we're not going to go to the lake at all. We're going to spend the rest of my visit sweltering in this itchy, sticky, chattering sauna.

"It's almost time to start a movie, Meghan! Hey, we should make vodka slushies today. You ever made those?"

"No, but I'll take it." I'll take anything wet. Especially if it numbs my brain. Connie stops talking, just for a moment, so I say, "How come you moved away from Sherwood Park anyway?"

Age fourteen. Connie writes to Janice and me from Vauxhall, Two Hills, Cold Lake—places I've never heard of. Pages and pages in her careful, neat handwriting about the town and the new friends and the softball tournaments she's in. Connie, who had hardly any friends and never played any sports when she lived on my street.

Connie twists her hair tighter and tighter. "My stepdad took my brother Ken and me to the High Level Bridge in Edmonton." She looks hard at Amber. "Hold your Popsicle over your plate, Amber, you're dripping." She looks at me again. "He told us to jump," she says. And then her eyes look heavy, and she yawns.

"He told you to jump?"

"Dump!" Amber yells, and jumps up and down. I start to laugh. Connie's frowning, so I squeeze my lips together hard and look away.

I wait to see what Connie will say next. She just looks over at me with wide-open, glassy eyes. Like she's just woken up. "What did you do?" I ask.

"Well, I didn't jump, did I? Duh. We left. Mom and Ken and me. Didn't tell him where we went. You and Janice were the only ones who knew." She gets up and walks into the kitchen.

Amber scoots across the floor and climbs onto my lap. She pops her thumb into her mouth and twirls my hair around her finger. Floppy floppy rag doll. I hug her tight, but not too tight, not like Connie hugged me.

In a few minutes Connie's back carrying a metal tray with a big bowl of popcorn and three tall glasses of Coke. "Dinner," she says, and puts the tray on the coffee table. "Ours have rum in them." She raises her eyebrows a few times. "Girls' night out, hey? Stove doesn't work, too hot to cook, what're two girls gonna do? Can't make slushies—I forgot to make ice, can you believe it?" She lets out a hard laugh, like it's the funniest thing. Then all of a sudden she's serious again. "Back to your chair, Amber. She'll manipulate you, Meghan. She knows what she's doing."

"She's not, Connie."

Connie glares at me and I feel as if it's me she's told to sit in that little chair. I look away. We eat popcorn and gulp our rum and Coke. I can't believe how thirsty I am.

"Hey, you still have a crib board?" I ask. "You play with Rod?"

"Are you kidding?"

Connie takes Amber down the hall to her bedroom. I go along and stand in the doorway while Connie pulls off Amber's dress and changes her diaper. Connie puts her in the crib just like that and tells her to go to sleep.

"Girls' night at last!" Connie says on the way back to the living room. She holds up a video.

"*Porky's*? I hear it's pretty dumb."

"Have you seen it?"

"No."

"Then don't knock it. You can pick the next one."

We sit on the couch. Connie starts the movie and we hear a quiet whimper from down the hall.

"That's just her," Connie says. "That's how she falls asleep. Just ignore her."

"Where's Rod?"

"He'll be around."

I can't help listening to Amber. She's gone from whimpering to talking to herself to humming and finally to silence. After the silence has gone on for some time I begin to relax. In the middle of the movie, Connie goes to the kitchen for more rum and Coke. She lights a cigarette.

"It's weird, Connie. We're basically adults now. You don't have to root through closets. You can just go buy cigarettes. We don't have to hide stuff. Doesn't it feel weird?"

"What are you talking about?"

"What we used to do. Steal your mom's stuff. Steal other stuff. Smoke in your bedroom so no one saw."

"I never stole anything. Is that something you did with Janice?" She starts the movie and looks away, at the television. She looks mad again, so I don't say anything else.

The movie is about as dumb as the ones we used to watch, but for some reason we find it funny. At first it feels strange, laughing at something so dumb, but after a while it doesn't feel strange at all, probably because we're not really paying attention and don't know what we're laughing about. The movie ends and even that cracks us up.

"How can this be funny?" I ask.

"It's not, but you're a riot. I'm making more popcorn. You pick out a movie," Connie says.

I nearly fall over when I get off the couch. "Connie, I can't stand up!"

"Ha ha, I'll make yours a little stronger next time," Connie calls from the kitchen.

I kneel down to read the titles scrawled in black felt pen on the sides. *Rocky III. War Games. Blade Runner.* Some are just marked with an X. Finally I pick *Halloween.*

"*Halloween?* I hear it's pretty dumb," Connie says, mimicking me.

"Yeah, yeah," I say.

We settle onto the couch with the popcorn. We laugh so hard our sides ache and we can't hear the movie. Toward the end I figure out why I keep laughing: it takes away the strangeness I feel around Connie.

The porch door bangs open.

"It's the Rodster," Connie says. She crams a handful of popcorn into her mouth.

All my neurons have detached. "Who the heck is the Rodster?"

"Rod."

He walks in and leaves the door between the living room and the porch open. Then he stops in front of me with his legs spread wide like a cowboy's. "You must be the famous Meghan," he says, kind of slow and drawn out, as if it's a speech he practiced. A strong smell comes off him, some mix of beer and smoke and sweat and the hot, dusty streets. "Come all this way to see your old friend Connie, eh? Pleased to make your acquaintance." Before I can say anything, he saunters down the hall to the big bedroom and calls back, "How's Amber?" He comes back a few seconds later and pulls off his white-and-black AC/DC T-shirt and tosses it onto a kitchen chair. "Christ, what a heat wave. What is there to eat?" He opens the fridge and grabs a can of beer. He cracks it open and guzzles half the can, then pushes the fridge door shut with his foot.

I look sideways at Connie without turning my head. She's not moving either. I wait to see what she'll say.

"You're lookin' at it," Connie says at last. Her forehead is tight and screwed up like she has a headache.

"Don't talk to me like that!" Rod snarls. He comes across like he is playing at being a cruel husband, the way Connie is playing at being a mom and having her own house. It's funny and not funny at the same time. "Whatever," he says. "I ate at Jason's. His wife knows how to cook." He takes another long swig of beer.

I'm about to whisper to Connie about how mean that was, but before I say anything one of the kittens runs into the house through the open door. I expect Connie to ream Rod out but instead she gets up and goes to the kitchen.

"What in hell are you doing in here?" Rod yells. The kitten skids on the kitchen floor, cowers under the table and pees. Rod pulls it up by the back of the neck and stomps dramatically to the porch, lifting his knees high. He holds the kitten way above his head and opens his hand so the kitten drops to the porch floor. The kitten lands with a thud and squeals. "Damn son of a—"

"Hey!" I yell. "What are you doing?"

Rod looks over at me and grins. "What am I doing? What am I doing, you ask? Training a cat, for God's sake. You liked that? Want to see it again? Works like a damn."

I shake my head.

"Kittens can handle a little roughness," he goes on, staring hard at me. "So," he says to Connie, "didn't you buy any food?"

"You didn't give me any cash," Connie says, so softly I don't think Rod can hear. She brings the rum and Coke from the kitchen and tops up our glasses before sitting down.

"Don't, I'll barf," I say.

Rod is walking down the hall again. "How 'bout you get a job, ha ha," he calls. "Or learn to cook." The bedroom door slams shut, so hard the velvet lion on the wall gives a shudder.

Connie shakes her head and says, "Don't worry about it, it's just him. Guys are like this. You'll see. You have a boyfriend? I'll hook you up with someone."

"Yes," I say, just so she won't hook me up with someone.

Rod saunters back. He opens the porch door, drops his empty beer can on the floor, and stomps hard on it before tossing it onto the pile of beer cans. He goes to the fridge to grab another beer and then sits down between us, pushing my hip hard against the side of the couch.

"Think you can clean that porch tomorrow, sweetheart?" Rod makes sweetheart sound like a dirty word. He brings his beer to his lips, tips his head back, and glugs until he's drained the can. "You like the TV, Meghan? Brand new." He smacks his lips and moves his face so close to mine I'm blasted with beer breath.

"Go away, Rod. This is our girls' night." Connie pushes at him. "I was sitting beside Meghan."

"Come on, will ya," Rod whines. "You've seen this movie a million times."

"I told you Meghan was coming. You don't have to ruin everything."

"It's not me that ruins everything," Rod says. "I didn't say she could come." He clamps his mouth shut, but his body is so wound up I know he's not done. I wait, and wait some more, and finally he jumps up and yells "Fuck it!" and stomps down the hall to the bedroom and slams the door.

Connie sighs. "I'll go talk to him. I don't want him to stay

angry. I'll be back." She walks slowly down the hall and into
the bedroom and closes the door.

First, I hear a yelp, then scuffling sounds. And the house
is quiet. I get up, listening hard, ready to run. After a minute I realize I'm holding my breath. A shriek comes from the
television, and I jump. I remember Amber jumping around
the room, how it was funny and not. I turn the television off
and go through the covered porch to the front steps. It's late,
after eleven, maybe even past midnight. The air is heavy and
hot. I'm covered with Popsicle juice and sunscreen and dust
mixed with sweat and rum and beer and smoke and some
other thing, some deep, heavy feeling I can't name. I want the
lake, how I want to be in the lake, to wash it all away.

A breeze slides across my skin and lifts the hairs on my arm.
I go inside and take the glasses and the popcorn bowl with
its few unpopped kernels to the kitchen and stare at the sink
full of glasses and cutlery. I hear television sounds and loud
talking from the house next door, not the furniture-throwing
house but another one, and a baby crying somewhere, a baby
with a hard, raging cry, and then a siren starting up. The velvet
lion snarls down at me.

I move closer to the little shelf of knick-knacks. They're
the same ones Connie had when she lived on my street—the
wooden rocking horse, the plastic doll in the Swiss dress, the
Japanese fan, tightly closed, the round deck of playing cards
in a plastic box. I take each one in my hand and set it down
carefully. These things are the Connie I used to know. I feel
like I'm touching Connie, touching something that's buried
deep inside her. Or used to be.

"Hey," Connie says. She's crept up behind me. Her hair is
mussed and her face has red blotches on it. She wears a thin
baby blue bathrobe, and she holds out bed sheets and a turquoise blanket. "Let's make your bed." She smiles. A real smile,
even through the blotches.

"Is it okay to stay?" I whisper.

"Huh?" Connie looks confused and hurt and sad, all at once.
"Why not?"

"Rod…"

"What?"

I don't want to tell her I'm scared stiff, but she figures it out.

"Oh. Well." She frowns and looks away. "You're fine. Come on, take this sheet." She hands me one end without lifting her eyes to look at me.

We don't say anything, making the bed. After she goes, I turn off the ceiling light and lie down on top of the blanket in my shorts and T-shirt. My eyes are open for a long time.

A car horn wakes me a little after eight o'clock. I'm still on top of the blanket. The air is already warm, and the sunlight stings my eyes. There's a throbbing inside my head. Amber coos and sings. I want to get her. But I fall asleep again. Much later, close to ten, Connie comes out of her room, in her blue bathrobe.

"Hey," she says on the way to the kitchen. "You drink coffee?

"Yeah." I get up and move Rod's T-shirt and the *Cosmo Girl* magazines from the chair to the table and sit. My head is heavy.

Connie fills the coffee pot with water. "I'll be going to work soon. Once I get my high school." She speaks slowly. She's as fuzzy-headed as I am. I see the empty rum bottle on the counter. That much rum. I want to throw up. "I was bored. So I never finished. Rod, he's the best thing that happened to me—same crazy sense of humour I have, you can tell, can't you. What do you take in your coffee? We love Slave Lake. Public health is a pain, though. About Amber. Not much work here yet. For me. We haven't met many people, but we will. It's only been a year. A year and a bit. Maybe two. Everything blurs together after a while, you'll see, when you have yourself a man and a baby. You drink coffee?" The coffee starts to drip. "I can go a bit crazy when Rod is gone a lot. I mean, when he's gone and when I'm on my own. See what I do?" Connie shows me odd red marks on her forearms. "The doctor says it's a sign."

"Of what?"

"That's what the doctor said. How would I know? I'm not the doctor. Milk or sugar?" Connie pours coffee into two mugs. "You said coffee, right?"

"Yes, coffee, with milk. A little sugar."

"I'm bigger than Rod, but he's stronger. All muscle. You lose your muscle when you have a baby, Meg, you know that?"

"No." I take the coffee.

"You're different, Meghan. You've changed."

"What?" Of course I have. It's Connie who hasn't. She's just the same as she was five years ago. She's not grown-up, like Janice and me. Weird, because Connie had all the grown-up ideas and games when we were younger, and back then she seemed so grown-up to me. But she was just a kid trying to be grown-up. Same as now. She hasn't changed at all. For a moment I imagine I'm already home, telling Janice all of this.

A lawn mower starts up outside the kitchen window and roars past. Connie sits up straight and her eyes bulge out. "I can't believe someone is out mowing this early on a Sunday. Can you believe it! He'll wake the whole neighbourhood! What is wrong with these people?"

The mower stops. The kittens are mewling.

"Should I give them milk?" I ask.

Connie shakes her head. "It's not them. It's Amber." She puts two slices of bread in the toaster, then just stands there staring at it, so I'm the one who goes to Amber. When Amber sees me, she stretches out her arms and squeals happily and jiggles her legs. I peel the sopping diaper from her, Velcro a clean one snugly around her belly, and put her in a dress covered in red and yellow sunflowers. Then she climbs onto me, sweaty, her legs dangling and a finger twirling my hair. All the way to the kitchen she babbles nonsense words in her chirpy voice.

"Look who I found!"

Connie is spreading margarine on toast. "You should have left her there." She's miffed. "Till I was ready for her."

"But she's been awake for hours. And she was soaking wet."

"She's got you wrapped around her little finger. Just put her in her chair. Amber!" She hollers. "Get to your chair!"

I carry Amber to the little plastic chair and set her down. Her fingers move up to her ears and begin their flick-flick before she's out of my arms. I get my brush and pull it through the tangles. Then I see the blood on her fingernails. When I try to look at her fingers, Amber quickly sits on both hands. The blood comes from behind her ears—thin streaks of fresh blood on top of old scabs.

"Oh my God. Connie, did you see this?"

"See what?"

"Her ears."

"Yeah, she does that. Toast's on the table. Have some while it's hot."

"But doesn't she need a Band-Aid or some cream or something?"

"She knows she'll get in trouble for it. She chews her nails too. They're all ragged. I have to keep putting hot pepper on them." Connie takes a sip of coffee. "She knows better. Kids do these things." She looks at me like I'm a dolt and would know this if only I had a kid of my own.

An alarm clock whizzes past my head and crashes into the knick-knacks on top of the bookshelf. Everything on the shelf goes flying. The bedroom door slams and the lion slides up to the left.

Connie steps into the living room. She looks at the knick-knack shelf and doesn't say anything, but her whole face has gone soft like she's going to cry. I wish Janice were here. She would know what to do. I feel useless. I don't know where to put my hands. I don't know if it's okay to hug Connie. Connie turns back to the counter and spreads more margarine on her toast. It makes me gag.

"We're being too loud," Connie says. "He likes to sleep in. It's time I got rid of that stuff anyway. I'd better take you out somewhere."

Age fourteen. Connie and I get caught at the Red Rooster. Not Janice; she hasn't swiped anything today. The strange part is, Connie takes all the blame. She tells the store manager it's her idea, and he believes her. For some reason he doesn't call my parents. He just reams us out and lets us go. I didn't want you to get into trouble, Connie tells me when we get to her house. Later, Janice tells me the real reason Connie took the blame. If your folks know what's going on, she says, they won't let you hang out with Connie anymore.

Connie drives us to the truck stop café and we go in and she orders Cokes, three of them. The floor is sticky. The waitress hollers food orders to somebody in the back. *Apple pie with ice cream. Coffee fries no gravy.*

I've been tricked. The feeling washes over my body all at once. No Janice, no lake, no girls' night; just a lot of rum that made me sick. My head buzzes from the drinking and the talking and the heat. I slide my Coke can over an old coffee-ring stain on the gold-specked Formica, trying to fit the can's rim perfectly on the ring. Amber sits on my lap. She sucks hard on her thumb and twirls a strand of my hair in her finger.

"Will you send pictures of her?" I ask. What I really want to know is why Connie asked me to come. "At Christmas and her birthday?"

"We don't have a camera." She flicks her cigarette over the ashtray. Then, staring hard at the ashes: "Sorry about the lake, hey."

I look out at the highway, desperately hoping the bus will be early. Finally I say, without looking at Connie, "It's okay."

"You know, all those years, when we kept moving, you were the only friend I had," Connie says. Her voice is so low I almost don't hear. I keep my eyes glued to the highway and try to look relaxed. But I'm uneasy about what she will say. "That's why I kept writing. Rod told me you wouldn't come. He didn't even want you to come." Her voice is getting softer and deeper, almost rasping. "So when you—oh, look." There is the bus, a great grey mass turning into the dusty parking lot.

My skin feels thick from the heat. Maybe it's not heat at all, not heat or sweat or grime but the heaviness that comes with feeling that you've let someone down, even after all this time. Just before Connie moved, she told me that I would forget about her, we were so different. I told her she was wrong. But she knew, back when she took the blame at the Red Rooster. I don't know why it matters to me now, but it does. For the moment, it's all that matters.

I look at her and say, "I did write back."

Connie's eyebrows scrunch. She looks hard at me.

"I wrote to you. All the letters came back. You'd already moved." She doesn't need to know how small this grain of truth is or how carelessly I wrote a few words on loose-leaf paper. But for a second or two, the frown that's always on Connie's forehead goes away. Even the lines around her mouth. Washed way. Like she gets it. Then all the lines come back. Connie shakes me away with her head and hands as if to say, whatever. You'll be gone soon and you'll forget about me. Again.

I grab my duffle bag and walk outside. The bus spews hot diesel at us. I kneel down and reach out my arms to Amber. She sticks out her tongue, shoves her hands behind her back, and turns her whole body away. I stand and look at Connie. She stares at me with bright eyes and casually shoves her hands into her jeans pockets.

"Well. Call me sometime," she says. "You've got my number."

❧ IN THE MEADOW

Annie and Steve have moved six times. In the moves, they have misplaced the following: a mohair sweater. One blue shoe. The clock radio. Annie's favourite jeans. An entire box of old photographs, left to Annie in her mother's will. A tourist poster of Brazil. *Tirra Lirra by the River*—a book she'd found in a second-hand bookstore and bought because she liked the sound of the title. There are more things—Annie is sure there are more things she has lost, though she can't say what. She feels a hollowness from time to time. Every now and again she thinks of the sweater, the jeans, the book, even the poster, and wonders about the things that might be missing that she doesn't know about, can't remember.

"It's like they're little parts of me," she told Steve once, "that are gone forever and I'll never be a whole person again."

"Oh, you're so melodramatic, Annie. Of course you will," Steve said. "Look at you. You are whole. All over," he added with a chuckle.

This morning Annie says, "Why didn't I know, Steve?"

They're upstairs, in their room. Their bedroom is the entire top floor of the house, under the sloping roof. Annie doesn't like having to duck, but she likes everything else about it. Everything but the heat. There are two windows, one on each wall. Annie leaves the windows open day and night, thinking it will help cool things off. It's too hot up here, summer and winter. But she likes this room. It's two whole levels away from Ross and Gemma, who have taken over the entire basement.

Annie would like to lose those two in a move sometime. Gemma and Ross have lived with Annie and Steve for so many years Annie has lost count. Or she doesn't want to count. Ross and Gemma are with them for better or worse, Annie sometimes says. It was a joke at first, and she said it in a cheesy voice.

Now she rolls her eyes when she says it, and Steve gives her a little squeeze, if he's near her. A few years ago it was a playful squeeze. Now it's more like a pinch, meant to tell her to keep her thoughts to herself.

"Oh, Annie, enough," Steve says. "I'm heading down now. They're waiting for me." He ducks under the roof and takes off down the stairs.

Steve and Ross met when they were tree planting in northern Saskatchewan. They work, Steve and Ross and Gemma, planting trees in the summer or sorting mail during the Christmas rush or sometimes as cooks for those camps in remote areas, and then they go on EI for a while, and then work again, round and round. For weeks at a time they are gone and the house is quiet and eerie and strange-feeling and Annie thinks there are bugs crawling up her arms when there aren't, or she hears sounds, a thump or a bang, and is too frightened to have a look. She wasn't always like this. It happened slowly. It's why she got the dog. So she wouldn't be alone.

It can be too quiet when they're home, too. They're all home now with their butts glued to the kitchen chairs. Annie sees them when she steps into the kitchen after Steve. He straddles the closest chair.

"Your deal," Ross says. He shoves the deck of cards toward Gemma. This is about as much as any of them ever says. Sometimes they chuckle or mutter "pass" or nudge each other or howl in protest about something, but mostly they don't say anything. And they don't like Annie talking to them when they're deep in a game. Especially when it's poker.

"Oh, Annie, you're here," Ross says. "C'mon, Annie, play with us!"

Annie smiles. He asks at least once a day. The others almost never ask. They've given up. Ross knows she won't play so it's become a little joke between the two of them. She smiles long enough to let him know she enjoys it, he can keep up his end of the little game.

Gemma straightens her stack of pennies. It's long, like her neck. Annie thinks of the long neck-rings some African women wear. How the neck eventually becomes weakened from them—if you took the neck-rings away, the women would not be able to hold up their heads. Her grandmother told her this.

"Annie, get some beer, will you," Steve says. He's looking at the cards splayed in his hand. "When you go for groceries."

Annie is staring out the window into the backyard. "Why didn't I know something was wrong?"

"Get off it, will you, Annie," Steve says. He takes a card from his hand, looks at it for a few seconds, and then inserts it in a different place.

"It wasn't obvious," Ross says, looking over at her. "There was nothing you could have done."

"Did any of you notice anything?" Annie asks.

The silence is unbearable. Finally, Ross says, kindly, "No, Annie. We told you. She was fine. We miss her too."

Annie looks down at the empty water bowl and the food dish. She hasn't been able to move them yet. Then she grabs Saturday's paper, yesterday's, and reads aloud: "Killer drunk driver admits guilt. Driver mows down four in Calgary, killing three." She pauses. "Video lottery terminal petition imminent. Albertans spend an estimated $600 million on VLTS since same time last year. WHO warns of one billion death toll from smoking—"

"What the hell?" Gemma turns to Annie and makes a face.

"You going?" Steve asks.

"Annie, you have to stop reading that stuff," Gemma says. "It's so morose. I feel morose just looking at you. You should watch a good comedy. Or a chick flick. Want to see a chick flick tonight?"

"My dog died," Annie says. She gives Gemma a look that says, You don't get it, and walks out to the car.

Annie stops at Safeway first and pulls out her list. She doesn't know what she'd do without her list, today; she can't think what they need. She's not hungry. She hasn't eaten much in the last week. The list reads: bananas, milk, bread, carrots. And at the bottom, in Steve's scrawl: *Don't forget the hot dogs.* BEEF! Annie smiles. Before Ross and Gemma, the short, short time before Ross and Gemma, or just *before*, as Annie likes to say to Steve when they're alone, when Annie and Steve were a couple and did couple things together, boarder-less, they'd go to the park in the ravine and roast weenies, and Steve would razz Annie for getting the ones with cheese or mesquite or pork, anything a little different. Boarder-less. She likes that. *Before*, she didn't have to think about which cupboard was hers and which half of the fridge and where she should sit and when she could speak so she didn't interrupt the game and whether she and Steve were a couple still.

She moves through the fresh produce, the bakery, the dairy; she avoids the pet-food aisle altogether. When she gets to the processed meats she decides to skip the hot dogs and go to the liquor store instead. Things seem to go better all round when they've had a few beers. Ross and Gemma, they're supposed to pay for their own, chip in, and Steve tells Annie they always do, but Annie isn't sure.

When she gets home they're still at the kitchen table, just the way they were when she left, elbows on the table, shoulders slumped, eyes on the cards. Silent. Talking with their eyes or a wave of the hand or a tipping of one finger—a code she's stopped trying to decipher. Some of it, she suspects, has nothing to do with the card game they are playing. She unloads the groceries and then goes back for the beer and puts a few in the fridge.

Ross has the most pennies. Ross is sweet looking and smart and sometimes a little lost in his own world. Fair hair, blue eyes, freckles when he's been out in the sun for too long. Good old what-you-see-is-what-you-get Ross from Saskatoon.

"Hi," Annie says finally. "Beer's in the fridge."

"Hi, you're back." Ross waves in her direction. "Gonna play now?"

"Play with us, Annie," Gemma says. She puckers her lips at Annie. "Pretty please."

Gemma has long, curly hair, long fingernails, long legs, a long nose. Lipstick, mascara, powder, blush. It's a mask. She's like the models in the art class Annie and Steve took *before*. Steve has more talent, Annie believes. Annie gave up drawing when she took the job in Student Records at the university. She's been there forever now, it seems, mindlessly entering names and addresses and birthdates. Steve is still drawing, when he's not treeplanting or cooking. Or playing cards. They moved to this place, an old one-and-a-half-storey, so that he could have more space to draw. The moves are always like that: Steve wants more room or lower rent or a bigger yard. The spare room on the main floor is his alone; Annie never goes in there. She hasn't seen him work in a long time, though.

"No, thanks," Annie says. "I have lots to do." She goes upstairs, pulls the sheets off the bed and tosses them into the laundry hamper, then opens the wardrobe near the window and pulls out fresh linens, the thin green ones. She loves the feel of new sheets, the coolness of them. A breeze passes over her when she flings the fitted sheet over the bed. "Sandy," she says quietly. "Sandy, Sandy, Sandy."

She tucks in the top sheet. She can never make it line up evenly without going from side to side several times to make sure it isn't hanging down more on her side than his. This is one of her least favourite activities, though she's made beds for years—first her mother's bed, then her younger sisters' and brothers,' all seven beds, until her sisters finally did their own. Annie is the oldest. And the odd one. Her mother never told her she was beautiful; and she wasn't brain material, her mother said, so she'd better go and learn a trade to support herself. And then when Steve came along, her mother practically pushed her out the door, saying, "You won't find a better guy than Steve, now go, go before he changes his mind." Her face had looked both desperate and relieved. As if no one would want Annie, her odd one. My scrawny little one, her mother used to call her.

Good sheets. Annie adds this to her mental list of things that go missing when she and Steve move. She doesn't know how it's possible to lose so many things.

Annie changes into a sleeveless shirt and shorts, smoothes the bedspread and sits on the bed, pulls her hair into a ponytail, twists it into a bun. She hates her hair, this long, thick hair that she never knows what to do with. The air is hot and unbearably still. She looks down at the floor beside her feet, where Sandy should be, resting her head on Annie's foot and looking up at her. She wishes she could cry.

"The boys are out back," Gemma says. She's come up the stairs without making a sound.

Annie gets up quickly, startled, and goes to the window that overlooks the side yard where Sandy was buried. There's the mound, still fresh. Steve and Ross stand beside it, hands in their jeans pockets, their backs to the mound, like it's not there. Steve has one foot on an old soccer ball.

"What's up?" Gemma asks.

Everything was fine till last Tuesday, Annie wants to say. Sandy got up, ate, even had a walk with me, our usual walk through the ravine to the dog meadow. "My dog died," Annie says. What she wants to say is that Sandy loved her.

"Everybody knows your dog died. Get over it. You'll get another dog."

What Annie means is nobody loved her the way Sandy did.

"Don't you think they look like brothers?" Gemma asks.

Steve passes the ball to Ross with the inside of his right foot and Ross boots it back.

"What?"

"You know how people start to look like each other or talk like each other when they're around each other a lot? Like dog owners and their dogs, ha ha!"

Annie would rather be downstairs, in the kitchen or the yard, with the guys around. She doesn't like the feeling Gemma gives her.

"Hey, Annie," Gemma says, in a soft, velvety voice. "D'you feel, you know, married?"

Oh, no, Annie thinks. Gemma and Ross will never move out. Never.

"I mean, have you—" Gemma looks around the room. "I

mean, take Ross. On some days I could take him or leave him, you know," she says in the same silky voice. "We talked about getting married a while back but, oh, I don't know." She sweeps the thought away with a flick of her hand. "Once I was at a bridal shower where the bride received fourteen knives. Fourteen, Annie!"

Annie starts down the stairs. "I'm going to do the dishes."

Their dishes are there, the breakfast plates and cups. Annie hates the mess more than the act of cleaning up after everybody. She washes the dishes, leaves them in the rack to dry, and makes some fruit salad. She hears Gemma slip down to the basement. Steve comes in from outside.

"Want some lunch?" Annie asks.

"Sure," Steve says.

Annie is looking for the yellow bowls, the two yellow bowls she'd found at a garage sale. Her mother had given her a set of china from Superstore when she moved in to Steve's place, *before*. A wedding gift, her mother said, though there'd been no wedding, just a quick visit to a JP, meant to be a temporary thing until they could decide what kind of wedding they'd have. Annie didn't want that many teacups and bowls and plates, big ones, small ones, too many. We're not an army! she told her mother.

There at the back of the cupboard are the yellow bowls. Not lost after all. Annie breathes out deeply, relieved.

"I made fruit salad," Annie says.

"Steve, we're dealing!" Ross shouts from the porch. "Hurry up!"

"You coming, Steve?" Gemma calls.

Steve takes the bowl and walks outside.

In a few minutes Annie joins them with her fruit salad and some iced tea and an old *Country Living* magazine. They're at the picnic table, the three of them. Annie sits off to the side in the deck chair under an old umbrella.

"Come play," Ross says.

Annie smiles and shakes her head.

"How come you never play?" he asks.

"Just don't," Annie says.

Gemma cranes her long neck toward Annie. "Any of that fruit left?"

"That was it."

"That was it?" Gemma asks.

"You can buy your own damn fruit," Annie says. She opens the magazine at random and glances down at a cast-iron four-poster bed with a white Martha Stewart bedspread.

"What's up with you?" Steve asks.

Annie doesn't say anything.

"Her dog died, don'tcha know," Gemma says.

"Gemma," Ross says harshly. He tosses his cards on the table and gets up. "She didn't mean that, Annie. She's really sorry about your dog. We all are."

Annie's mad, but not at Ross, so she doesn't say anything back. She takes her bowl and glass inside and throws them into the sink, hard. The bowl, miraculously, doesn't break.

The day Sandy died, Annie had taken her along the path in the ravine before she went to work. Sandy trotted along beside her until they got to the dog meadow at the end of the ravine and then bounded off after one of the regulars. The labradoodle was there and the curly-haired white Russell terrier and the old grey mutt, all of them bouncing happily, wagging their tails, rolling in the grass, smelling butts, growling playfully.

What Annie liked about walking Sandy was that people talked to her. Whenever she's out with Steve, he does all the talking, and people talk to him without ever talking to her or even noticing her. She's so used to it by now that she stares off into the distance, thinking about other things, not expecting anyone to say anything to her. But at the dog meadow, everybody talked to her. At first, it was just about Sandy. They all wanted to know what she was, where Annie found her, how she came up with the name. Part golden retriever, Annie would say. An ad in the paper. Sandy-coloured. They all remarked on what an easygoing dog she was.

Steve didn't want a dog; Annie knew that before she began browsing through the ads. He didn't want to look after a dog, be tied down by it.

"I'll look after it," Annie said.

"You're a looking-after sort of person, aren't you?" He sounded curious.

"No," she said, not looking up. "I just want a dog."

At the dog meadow, everybody asked how she was doing and how work was and what was coming up on the weekend and if she'd seen the movie that just came out. If someone didn't show up or was late, Annie would feel a little unsettled, and throughout the day she would keep thinking about the person who didn't show up. And if Annie didn't show up one day, everybody would say to her the next morning, "Everything all right?" or "There you are, Annie! Missed you! Missed you and Sandy yesterday!" and she knew they did, her as much as Sandy.

The day Sandy died, Annie wanted to stay longer in the dog meadow, with the frivolity and bouncing and talk. She came home, though, where Steve and Ross and Gemma were all still sleeping, and slipped out again quietly, leaving Sandy out in the yard. Sandy died sometime during the day, but Steve didn't call her at work. He waited till she got home. Didn't want to wreck her day, he said. There was nothing she could do about it anyway, he said. He and Ross had already dug the hole, but they waited before burying her.

"What happened?" Annie asked over and over.

After a long time Steve said, "Think, think back to the walk, did she eat something?"

Annie remembered the garbage then, the loose garbage along the alley that Sandy nuzzled into and ate on the way home before she could pull her away. Maybe she had eaten something bad. They should have taken her to the vet, she said, why didn't they take her to the vet? Nobody had an answer. Annie called the vet herself, and the vet said Annie could bring her in, they could find the cause, but Annie didn't think there was any point. Sandy was dead.

Annie hasn't been to the dog meadow all week, but she thinks about going, every day. But who goes to a dog meadow without her dog.

Sunday night, Annie and Steve lie in bed naked, side by side on their backs, not close, the sheets and bedspread pulled back. When she moves her arm and her skin touches his, unintentionally, it burns. There's no breeze. Annie wishes they could have the basement in summer. She wishes they lived alone and could have the basement whenever they wanted.

"So," Steve says, "we've been talking, y'know, me and Gemma and Ross." His hands and fingers twist and turn as if he's trying to give shape to something he doesn't know the shape of. "Ross, he really likes you, you know he does. He keeps saying he'd like a more, oh, intimate relationship with you. And Gemma, she—"

"What?" Annie sits up and pulls her knees to her chest. She wants to feel less exposed. Something is coming that she needs to be ready for.

"Yeah." Steve puts a hand on her knee and she flings it off.

"I think I'll puke."

"Think about it, Annie. It could be good for you. Remember the first apartment?"

"Yeah. It was just us," Annie says in a husky voice. She remembers Sundays, not noticing the time till it got dark outside, their bodies fitting so well inside each other, feeling hot, pleasantly tired. Not wanting to move, massages, lying tucked in his arm or with her hand on his chest. Then, they'd have red wine and soft bread, French. Now, he chugs back beer on the back porch with his bowl of dill pickle chips. "Yeah," she says again. "I do remember."

"That was a long time ago," he says quietly. "Things have changed."

Annie pulls the sheet over herself and turns on her side, away from him. "For God's sake, don't talk like that, Steve. Don't talk like that."

In the morning she goes to work. It's a ten-minute walk. Trish at work knows about Sandy, had hugged Annie the day she learned Sandy died and for the rest of the week kept asking Annie how she was doing. This week Trish has forgotten about Sandy. She's talking about other things, asking about the rest of Annie's summer plans.

"We don't go anywhere," Annie says. "Steve never knows when he'll be around or for how long." What she means is that Steve won't leave Ross and Gemma.

"You remembered about the parade today?"

"What parade?"

"Downtown. We're closing early so we can all go if we want. Want to come?"

Annie shakes her head. "I'll just go home."

"You're such a homebody, Annie. Why don't you come?"

Annie shrugs.

She doesn't want to go home. She wants to be in the dog meadow but can't imagine herself there without Sandy. She walks slowly along the back alley to the yard. It's not a big yard, but it's big enough for a dog like Sandy. The yard has an eight-foot-high fence, old and needing repair. Some of the boards are warped or missing and there are gaps. Coming up to the fence, Annie can see, through a gap, Gemma on one side of the picnic table, Ross and Steve opposite. Gemma's long legs are stretched out in front of her. Steve is turned slightly inward, and his dark brown eyes are focussed on Ross, good old Ross who is sorting his cards.

Annie stops walking when she sees something moving

under the table. At first she thinks it's a stray cat, but then she sees that it's Steve's foot, sliding forward slowly till it rests on Gemma's. They're both barefoot. It's hot. Annie can't wait to take off the pantyhose she has to wear to work. Her blouse sticks to her back. A drop of sweat trickles between her breasts. The air is warm and dry and smells of something blooming nearby, the purple flower on the long stalk she can never remember the name of.

Gemma's other foot, the one not covered by Steve's, moves on top of his. Gemma's lips curl up, just a little, hardly at all really—so little that Annie thinks if she hadn't looked over right then, she wouldn't have noticed. Gemma's neck rocks forward a few times, as if she's keeping the beat to a tune that's come to her all of a sudden.

Annie pushes the back gate open and strides toward them.

"A little footsies under the table?" she wants to say. But she doesn't say anything. She prefers to barge right up to the table.

They drop their cards, all three of them.

"Jesus, woman, where'd you come from?" Steve sputters. He pulls his legs under the bench and sits up straight.

"You the invisible woman or something?" Ross chuckles. He's winning.

"How come you're home early?" Steve asks. "You get laid off?"

Gemma stares down at her hand. She won't look up at Annie. Her stack of pennies is short, off-kilter.

Annie kicks off her shoes and tosses them into the pile of sandals outside the door. All three pairs are in such a jumble that if Steve and Ross and Gemma stood in them, all six legs would be twisted around each other. She can almost see the legs, looking at the sandals. She gives them a kick that sends them scattering and walks inside.

"Annie," Steve says. He's come in after her. "Annie."

Annie goes up the stairs to her room and takes off her work dress and pantyhose. "Don't look at me," she says, her back to him. "Don't." She pulls on her shorts and T-shirt. "What's going on, Steve?" she asks. She looks in the mirror while she twists her hair into a loose bun. She wants to yank her hair out, all of it. "Why do they keep moving with us?"

"They have no place to go." Steve takes a few steps in her direction.

Annie shakes her head hard and her hair slips out of the bun. The hair makes her look old. When she was a teenager, a friend of her mother's came over and showed her two younger sisters how to put on makeup. They didn't ask her; they didn't think she'd be interested. "What's going on with you and Gemma?"

Steve slowly moves closer to Annie. "Geez, Annie." He tries to pull her up against him, but Annie wrenches herself away.

She feels cold, even up here. *Something in the coffee,* she thinks. She makes the coffee in the morning. *Arsenic.*

"I'd like them to go, Steve."

"Oh, Annie, don't start that again." He grabs his head. "Man, if you'd just stayed at work like you were supposed to! Don't bring this up again. They're staying."

Steve bounds down the stairs.

Annie arrives at the dog meadow sometime after five-thirty in the evening. They're all there, the mutts and mongrels, the black dog, the grey one, the shaggy pair. Annie looks out at the dogs, at the bouncing and leaping for balls and rolling on backs and mad wagging of tails. Then the voices come to her, all at once and tumbling over each other, like happy excited barking.

"Annie. Haven't seen you in ages!"

"It's Annie! I didn't recognize you—look at your hair! It looks great!"

"Annie! Long time no see!"

"Yeah, your hair, it's short. It suits you."

"Annie, where have you been? We've missed you."

"I've been busy," Annie says. "Moving and—"

"Where's Sandy?"

"Yeah, where's Sandy—I don't see her out there."

"Yeah."

"Annie."

"Oh, Annie."

"Sandy..." Annie says.

And suddenly they are all around her, close, some hugging, some wiping the tears that have finally come, some saying a few words, and then they are all talking about Sandy, and Annie can almost see the old girl bouncing along with the other dogs one last time, her tail wagging hard.

ꙮ TATTLETALE

Nobody said anything—not Ally, not Tom, not the little girl. Not Ally's brother, Mark, of course. He had run off right away. To tell, he had said. Ally closed her eyes and there looming large in her mind were Tracy's fat, squished-together red lips, her big, curly, brown hair, and the gigantic silver cross that hung from a heavy chain around her neck. Tracy was a nut. Anybody could see that. Ally's dad had known it last night, and he had never even met her.

Ally had heard her mom and dad talking about Tracy the night before. They were in the bathroom across the hall from Mark's and Ally's bedrooms. Ally could hear everything.

"That's a pleasant surprise, a visit from an old school friend," Dad said.

"It's a surprise all right," Mom said.

"Oh?"

"I haven't seen her in years, Nathan. I couldn't even tell you what she looks like. Anyway, it's the weirdest thing. She said she's coming to apologize," Mom said.

"For what?"

"I have no idea."

"How can you not know?"

"It was a long time ago. I don't remember much of it. She said she did some mean things. Oh, she said I wasn't sexy enough." Mom chuckled. "She said I'd never have a boyfriend. You know. Because Tracy and her little clique were allowed makeup and hair dye before the rest of us. Stupid things. All that crap you go through in high school."

"Sounds like a nut," Dad said into his toothbrush. "Why did you bother to let her come?"

They went into their bedroom next to the bathroom. Bits of the conversation made their way through the closed door. Mom saying she'd had a crappy day. That rude Mr. Watkinson was in again. Shhh, Dad said, shhh. And, Forget all that. There was more talking, low and deep, Dad's voice, too soft for Ally to hear. He was making Mom's day not so crappy. He always did that. No matter how bad Mom's day was, he made it better. All right, then, Ally heard Mom say after a while, All right. And then the moaning started. Sometimes Ally heard Mark slip out to the hall to hear better. Ally was embarrassed and put the pillow over her head. She wondered why it was always Mom who had the crappy day and Dad who tried so hard to make it less crappy. And there was something about the way Mom said "All right, then" that worked its way under Ally's skin and stayed there.

When Ally woke, the house was itchy all over. Itchy with the heavy heat of late July, itchy with little puffs of agitation in the air.

First came Mom's voice: "Oh, Lordy. Eggs. Don't we have any eggs?"

Then Dad's, impatient: "Lynn, there are eggs. I brought them home on Tuesday."

Mark slid past Ally's bedroom and gave her wall a thump. Then he slammed the bathroom door after himself. Night was over. Ally pulled on blue cotton shorts and her Calgary Stampede T-shirt and walked down the hall to the kitchen. The linoleum floor was cool on her bare feet. The kitchen smelled of coffee and toast and peanut butter. Mom was on the far side of the kitchen island, Dad in the front entrance, holding his summer jacket over his arm.

"Oh, there you are, Ally," Mom said. "Come and give me a hand. Where are the bananas?"

The big yellow mixing bowl was on the counter in front of her next to the bag of flour, the sugar, the eggs, the bananas.

"For Pete's sake, Lynn, the bananas are right there, beside the eggs," Dad said. He looked at his watch. He hated being late for work.

Mark stomped down the hall to the kitchen in his pajama bottoms. "Dad," he said. "I had my day planned. I was going to go to Drew's today. Mom wrecked my day."

"You'll go another day," Mom said. "Go get dressed and have something to eat."

"Grin it and bear it, son," Dad said. "Mother knows best. Chill." He looked over at Mom and smiled. "May the gods smile down on you today." He could go on like this for ten minutes if he needed to.

Mark looked glum and slunk back down the hall to his room.

"Well, Nathan," Mom said.

"Well," Dad said. It was the thing they said when they didn't know what else to say. "See ya later, alligator," he said in a singsong. "Toodle-oo." He blew Mom a kiss. The screen door banged shut after him.

The beaters shrieked for a few seconds. Mom turned them off and added eggs. The beaters shrieked again, then stopped. "Ally, I need the bananas. Don't just stand there. Tracy will be here any minute."

Ally peeled off the soft black skin and let the fruit fall into a bowl. She detested this job. She hated the smell and feel of overripe bananas, and when she mashed them, her nose crinkled at the sight of the pulpy mess. "Gross, Mom. Who's Tracy?"

"An old friend."

"When's she coming?"

"I don't know. Soon."

Mark stomped down the hall again.

"Mark, just look at you," Mom said. "Get dressed." Mark went back to his room without saying anything. Mom put the loaf pans in the oven. "Boys," she said. She smiled at Ally as if they were sharing a secret.

Some days, Mom said things like, "You boys and your boy energy. Shoo," and flicked Dad and Mark away with her fingers. "It's hell-thy, Lynn," Dad would say back, dragging out the *hell* in a phony ghoulish voice and giving her a fake evil grin. Or he'd say, "Boys will be boys." Ally hated boy energy. Boy energy came with boy meanness and boy jokes and, worst of all, boy smell. It seeped out of Mark and it seeped through the wall between their bedrooms. But boys somehow were not the same as boyfriends. Ally wanted to ask Mom why someone would say she'd never have a boyfriend, but then Mom would know she was listening to the nighttime conversations in the bathroom and would start having them somewhere else.

"Help me tidy," Mom said. "Tracy will be here any minute. I don't want her to see this mess."

"Everyone sees our mess."

"We know them."

Ally watched her wipe a small spot on the counter and then tuck a bit of hair behind one ear. And then wipe again. Wipe, tuck, wipe, tuck. She was bothered.

Ally ate cereal and then started for her bedroom. Mark watched through a tiny opening in his doorway. Ally knew what was coming. She moved slowly, sliding her back against the wall. He came out of his room and pretended to make for the bathroom and then lunged at her. He hooked his ankle around hers and tried to trip her, but she leapt onto his back and pulled his hair, hard, trying to get him down. He pinched her under the arms till she let go and then flung her to the floor and vanished into the bathroom.

Hot lava filled Ally's chest and surged through her arms and legs. She screamed Mark's name at the top of her lungs and then flopped onto her bed and breathed deeply. Her fingers found the mosquito-bite scab on her shin and picked at it. She used to like Mark. It wasn't just that his eyes had sleep gunk in them and he had pimples all over his face and his hair was greasy. It wasn't that he didn't bother to take showers or comb his hair and that he smelled like rotting meat half the time. It was that he'd become downright mean. He called her Baby or Little Princess and poked her in the side and laughed. If he was in a room with her for more than thirty seconds, he creeped her out either by looking at her for a long time without blinking—or by not looking her way at all.

The scab started to bleed. Ally sat up. Blood slid down her leg in a straight line. She waited till it got to her ankle and then pulled a Kleenex from the dresser, wiped the blood, and pressed hard on the scab.

Her three china dolls stared back at her from the dresser. They were propped up on stands, next to the ballerina jewellery box. "How are the children," Dad sometimes asked when he came to tuck her in. "How are Ally's children tonight?" He smiled when he said it, teasing. Maybe he thought she should be outgrowing them, she was too old for dolls. He didn't know they were for looking at, not for playing with.

Ally tossed the bloodied tissue into the plastic wastebasket beside the dresser and turned the key in the jewellery box. The pink plastic ballerina twirled in her puffed-out gauze dress while the mechanical insides clinked out *Swan Lake*. Ally used to twirl along with the ballerina. She stopped after Mark came in, gave a snort, and asked if her prince had come yet.

Ally heard footsteps and the *click-click* of heels on the front step. The doorbell rang and the front door opened and banged shut. Ally walked down the hall.

A woman and two children stood in the front entrance.

"Well, come in, Tracy," Mom said at last, though they were already in. They had let themselves in.

"Hello, Lynn, you look great," Tracy said, and then, "You must be Allison!" She clicked across the floor in her red heels and hugged Ally by touching Ally's shoulders with the tips of her fingers and leaning in a little. Her gigantic cross pendant whacked Ally in the neck.

"It's Ally," Ally said into Tracy's hair, and Tracy pulled back. Her eyelashes were coated with black mascara and her eyelids were painted in four different purply colours. She was tall and skinny and wore a bright-coloured flowery dress without any sleeves. She smiled the big red-lipped smile that Ally soon realized was stuck on her. Dad was right about her being a nut.

"And you're Mark," Tracy said. Mark had come up behind Ally so quietly she hadn't noticed. Tracy pointed at her children. "Tom and Crystal."

Tom was taller than Ally. Crystal looked like she was four years old. Ally knew from the way she stood up straight and looked hard at Ally that she was a demanding, bossy little girl. Tom looked…nice. His hair hung in his eyes, but it was washed. She looked all over for a pimple but couldn't see one. Ally felt cheated. In the natural order of things, she would end up with the little girl and Mark would end up with the boy. She racked her brains for the right thing to say so she wouldn't be stuck with the little girl.

"Tracy, I have banana bread," Mom said. She was walking back toward the island. "Banana bread just out of the oven. Just about to come out of the oven, I mean. I thought I was out of bananas this morning, then eggs. It was pretty funny, but there they were, ha ha."

"Mom," Ally said, wanting her to stop.

Mom frowned at Ally and turned to Tracy. "And coffee, fresh coffee. Do you drink coffee?"

"I hope you didn't make that for me. I have to watch what I eat or I just pack on the pounds," Tracy said. She said it like it was the funniest thing, but nobody laughed.

Crystal flipped her flowery sundress up and down over and over, lifting it higher each time till her frilly pink panties showed. "I like dolls," she said. "You got dolls? And princesses. And fairies, I got lots of fairies."

Ally and Mark and Tom looked at each other. Ally's arms felt long and heavy. She didn't know what to do with her hands.

"Do you have skim milk?" Tracy asked. "I'll just take it black if you don't. Don't go to any trouble for me. I'm so glad you agreed to meet me after, you know, after all this time."

Crystal twirled around and around in her sundress till she ended up at the loveseat in the little nook just off the kitchen. She flopped on it and kicked at the afghan till it slid onto the floor, and then she jumped up and skipped over to Ally.

"You got dolls?" she asked again.

"No," Ally said.

"Of course you do," Mom said. "Crystal, Ally's room is right down the hall."

Ally had a bad feeling about the little girl. She looked at Tom, desperately wondering what she should say so she wouldn't be stuck with his bratty sister, but then she walked down the hall after Crystal. When she got to her room, she saw that Crystal had pulled the red velvet dress off one of the china dolls. When Crystal saw Ally, she laughed hysterically and started to undo the doll's braids.

Tom had followed. He grabbed Crystal's arm and said, "Stop it!"

Ally yanked the doll away from Crystal and scooped up the other two. She held all three dolls against her chest. Mom and Tracy and Mark were in the hallway, looking in. Ally wanted them all to go away.

"What's going on?" Mom asked.

"She was wrecking the dolls," Tom said.

Tracy clicked into the room. "Allison, dear. She's just a little girl. You have to put away special things you don't want anyone to touch."

Tracy's pendant was at Ally's eye level. Ally thought the cross probably weighed five pounds. She figured it must give Tracy a headache. Ally started to get a headache looking at it.

"I'll tell you a secret," Tracy said. "I put my special things high up so Crystal can't reach. Come out, Crystal." She took Crystal by the hand and led her down the hall.

Mark glanced at Tracy's back and then pointed his finger in his mouth and gagged.

Mom followed Tracy back to the kitchen. "Tracy," she said, "we have toys downstairs that Crystal can play with."

Crystal pulled away from her mother and ran down to the basement.

"I'd better go with her," Tom said.

Ally laid her dolls on her bed and looked at them for a few seconds before going after him. Downstairs, Crystal had already dumped the huge Rubbermaid bin of plastic dinosaurs onto the carpet and was about to dump the box of coloured wooden blocks.

"Who's going to play with me?" Crystal demanded. She reached for the Lego tub.

"I have to play with her," Tom said. He knelt down. "At least some of the time. Don't make such a big mess, Crystal. You never clean up your messes."

Crystal ran up the stairs. "Mom!" she shrieked. "Mom! Tom's saying mean things to me!"

Tom rolled his eyes and then went up the stairs. Ally watched him go and then went back up after him. In the kitchen, Mom and Tracy were leaning against the counter by the sink. Mom listened and Tracy spoke quietly but with intensity.

"Mom!" Crystal yelled. She patted Tracy's arm. "Mom!"

"Children," Tracy said. "Lynn and I haven't seen each other in ages and we have some catching up to do. Maybe you could all go outside for a while. There's a park across the street. I can see it from here. Go on."

Mark slipped out the front door. Tom stood in the front entrance while Crystal painstakingly put on her sandals. "You have to wait for me, Tom," she said, looking up at him. "Mom says."

"What do you think I'm doing?" Tom asked.

"I'm ready!" Crystal jumped up and pushed open the screen door.

They crossed the street to the park. Mark sat down under a tree with his legs crossed and pulled out bits of grass. Ally and Tom sat down beside him and Crystal began to spin in circles in front of them.

"She's wearing a cross, like your mom," Ally said. "A tiny one."

Tom didn't say anything.

"You don't have one. How come they have crosses?"

Barely moving his lips, Tom said, "My mom was saved."

"Saved?" Ally had a sudden image of fire trucks and sirens and Tracy being pulled out of a burning house. She didn't know where Tom or Crystal were in this picture. Maybe in the house too.

"Let's go to the river," Tom said suddenly. "My mom said you live near a river."

Ally and Mark glanced at each other, and then at Tom. The

river was out of bounds. Mark's eyes lit up. He stood and started to walk purposefully. Ally and Tom and Crystal followed—slowly at first, but after a few seconds they all broke out into a run. They ran down the street and along the next one to the top of the valley, and then onto the dirt trail. The trail wound its way through the woods and eventually came out on the paved path. Here they all slowed, to catch their breath.

After a few minutes they left the main path and bushwhacked through the hazelnut bushes and Saskatoons and slid down a steep slope to the rocky river flats. Crystal ran in wide circles, stopping every now and again to pick up a stone and put it in her pocket.

Ally saw that Tom's and Mark's shirts were covered with burrs, on their shoulders and arms. For no reason she started to giggle.

"Hey!" Mark kicked pebbles at her. "What's so funny?"

"Yeah," Tom said. "What's so funny?" And, maybe because Mark had done it, he kicked pebbles her way.

Ally took a step back. "Your shirts," she said.

"What about yours?" Mark said. He started to pull at her shirt, and then she noticed that she'd picked up burrs too. Tom began to pick at them too. Ally felt a little pinch each time they got a burr. After they'd pulled the burrs off her shoulders they started to pick burrs off her chest. Ally whacked their arms and they stopped.

The three them walked slowly along the river flats, bumping into each other. Ally was in the middle. Mark gave her a bump and a push that sent her toward Tom, and he bumped her back to Mark. It was fun, at first, but when they began to push too hard, she dashed forward. Crystal ran to catch up with them, holding her full pockets from underneath.

Tom stopped near the water. The river was low and slow and muddy.

"What church do you go to anyway?" Ally asked.

Tom didn't answer.

"What's it like?"

Crystal looked at Ally. Then she inhaled deeply and hollered all in one breath: "You have to always be good and see just the good things that happen to you and pray every night for forgiveness and always tell your mother and father the truth!" Her nose seemed to grow more pinched and sharp as she spoke. "God knows when you lie." She narrowed her eyes at Ally when she said this, as if to say, And you *do* lie.

"Oh, be quiet, Crystal," Tom said. "That's what I hate about it."

"What?" Ally asked.

Tom gave a little shrug and picked up a stone. "What she just said. All of it," he said.

Ally found a flat stone, skipped it over the surface of the water, and silently counted five skips. Mark skipped a stone seven times. Tom watched them and then tossed his own stone. It sank as soon as it hit the water. Ally started to giggle but stopped when she saw how hard he was concentrating. He tried another stone, and then another, and every one was sucked into the river before skipping once.

"Like this!" Ally said. She skipped a stone halfway across the water. Tom made a face and pushed her—not hard, not the way a brother pushed. It was a push that said, Push me back. Ally gave a gentle push and giggled and then sprinted off a few feet, out of reach.

There was no one else by the river, Ally suddenly realized. It was quiet and strange. She stopped moving and looked around slowly. Crystal sat beside a large flat stone and stacked pebbles. Mark stood by the edge of the river, skipping stones. Tom strolled over to the bank and sat down under the overhanging shrubbery. Ally made her way over and sat beside him.

All she wanted was a little kiss, just to see what it was like— and because she did not want to be like her mother and have everyone say she didn't have a boyfriend. If anyone at school asked, she could say the boyfriend was Tom, even though he lived in another city. Tom was a nice enough boy. She moved forward and gave him a quick kiss on the lips, so quick she didn't feel anything.

Tom's eyes had looked half asleep before, but now they opened wide. He moved in close and gave her a hard kiss on the lips, then moved back and looked at her. Ally was about to say stop, but Tom came back and pushed in his tongue this time. Ally wanted to gag and pull away. His mouth was slimy. If she had gotten the chance, she would have said that all she wanted was one little kiss and they could carry on skipping stones. But he didn't take his lips off hers. She wondered if this was what happened after her mother said to her father, "All right, then." She wondered if this was why her mother moaned, because she couldn't breathe, and then she thought of Mark, listening outside the door. Mostly, she wanted to ask Tom what he was trying to do, but she knew that if she asked, he would know that she had no idea about anything at all. That was worse than not knowing what he was doing. So she lay back and waited for him to finish.

"Hey!" Mark was there. He flung himself on Tom and pushed him away. Tom leapt up. Mark hooked him around the neck and tried to force him down. Instead, Tom got Mark to the ground and wrestled with him till Mark yelled "Stop!"

"I'm telling!" Mark said. He glared hard at Ally. "You're in for it now." He scrambled up the bank and disappeared through the trees.

Ally looked at Tom and then quickly turned away. They both stared at the ground. Neither one said anything. Ally started slowly back toward a path out of the river flat. Tom moved along a few steps behind her.

"Crystal," Ally said, remembering, and turned back. Crystal was a long way behind them, wading along the shore, up to her waist in the water. Tom ran over to her and grabbed her hand and started yelling at her.

Crystal bawled like a baby for about five minutes and then began to complain. She didn't want to go. Her dress was too heavy. Her legs were tired.

Ally wondered what Mark would tell and why she was in for it. Her face was burning. She felt embarrassed and didn't know why. She wanted to ask Tom if she was his girlfriend now.

She wanted to say she was sorry about Mark jumping on him. But she didn't say anything.

"I want a carry," Crystal whined.

"No," Tom said. "Don't be such a baby."

"Sorry about your clothes," Ally said, finally, because she felt she should say something. His shorts had a rip and his shirt was covered in dirt from wrestling with Mark. "I hope you don't get in trouble."

"What do you care?" Tom said. "You started this, but I'll get all the blame." He didn't say anything more after that. Even Crystal was quiet.

When they got home, Tom persuaded Crystal to leave her pebbles on the front step. He took her down the hall to the bathroom.

Mom and Tracy were sitting on the back deck. Ally walked toward the screened porch doors and then stopped and watched them. There were two green coffee cups on the small table beside them. Mom was holding a plate with a piece of banana bread.

"Dan Wallace. I remember him. He was just a boy," Mom said. "Oh, come on, Tracy, we were kids. It was so long ago."

"We made you two go out that time. On a date. Don't you remember?"

"Tracy, it doesn't matter. Really."

"But we watched. You were in that crawl space, and we watched."

Mom put the plate down on the table, hard. When she spoke, it was like she had no air. "Enough, Tracy. We were kids. It's past. Let's leave it now."

Tracy turned to Mom with huge eyes and whispered: "We didn't know it was your first time. We were all there. Even that new boy, what was his name?"

Mom got up quickly and started toward the screen doors. "Ally!" she said. "You're filthy! Wash up and have some banana bread." Her cheeks were red and shiny. "Get out of those clothes." She stepped inside and walked with Ally toward the kitchen. Her eyes narrowed and she swore softly under her breath.

Ally went to her room and closed the door and undressed. So. Mark had not said anything. She listened for sounds of Mark coming from his room but didn't hear anything. When, then, and what? she wondered. She pulled on other shorts, another shirt. Mark must be waiting till Tracy goes home—then he'll tell. That's it.

The bathroom door was still locked. Ally went to the kitchen, washed her hands at the sink, and took a slice of banana bread. She sat at the table and picked off bits. She scrunched her nose, remembering mashing the slimy bananas for Mom and feeling all over again Tom's sloppy wet lips pushing hard against hers.

Tracy was inside now, too. Tom and Crystal came down the hall from the bathroom.

"Look at you," Tracy said. "How did you get so grubby? I'm sure Lynn doesn't want us tracking mud into her house."

Crystal climbed onto a seat beside Ally and grabbed a piece of banana bread. Tom sat down at the other end of the table from Ally and stared at his hands.

Mom stood by the island with her fingers pushed against the side of her head the way she did when she had a headache. Mark walked up to the table and grabbed two slices of banana bread. He sat down across from Ally and looked at her while he chewed.

"Thank you for letting me come," Tracy said. "Now I can move on."

Mom looked up at her. "Yes. You can."

Ally stared at Tracy's pendant. Then she looked at the kitchen clock and wondered when they would go. When they left, she'd slip into her bedroom and lie down and wait for Mom and Dad to talk, at bedtime. Tonight they'd talk about Tracy the nut again. They'd make a joke about her and have a good laugh.

🦅 NEW SUMMER DRESSES

It was the middle of August and hot and dry, and the air was filled with the *fleek-fleeks* of grasshoppers and the crackling of seed husks opening in the heat. With each step Mara and Anika took, grasshoppers exploded into the air around them. Mara and Anika were used to this, but Odine and Pierre were not. Odine and Pierre, who were visiting, cried out in surprise whenever a cloud of grasshoppers flew up at them, Odine especially. Mara and Anika thought she was funny. They loved her, too. They loved everything about her. When she caught up to them, they each took one of her hands.

Mara and Anika had light brown hair and blue eyes, and today, they wore matching summer dresses, a gift from Odine. The dresses were thin and sleeveless and covered in bright splashes of pastel pink and yellow and blue. They made the girls feel grown-up. On first glance the sisters looked alike, but they were not. The older girl, Mara, was lean and muscular. She was impatient and even a little impulsive. Anika had some baby fat still and tended to dawdle, which irked Mara at times. Sometimes Anika would stop to investigate a small movement in the grass or pick alfalfa, or she would take time selecting the right colours: purple and pink, no yellow. Mara, annoyed, would say, "Hurry, Anika, come on." But today, Anika didn't dawdle. Today, both girls wanted to be close to Odine.

Pierre took Anika's other hand, yelled, "Un...deux...trois... wheeeee!" and he and Odine swung Anika high in the air.

"Now me," Mara said, and switched places with Anika.

"Go easy on Pierre," Mara's father said. He walked beside their mother and carried a willow basket full of towels and cookies and wine.

"Don't worry," Pierre said. He lifted his big black camera, which hung from his neck, up to his face and aimed it straight ahead. *Click-click*, said his camera. *Click-click-click*.

Pierre and Odine were not yet parents and seemed very young and mysterious to Mara and Anika. Odine looked like she was straight out of a fairy tale. She had a smattering of freckles on her cheeks and what their mother called straw-berry-blonde hair. Her face was almost always lit up in a smile and she scooped up both girls frequently to "steal" hugs and kisses; she read to them and told them stories in the cabin at night and, most magical of all, sang to them in French. Pierre made them laugh with his attempts to make sense of every-thing at the cabin; he asked the wood stove and the rain bar-rels long, elaborate questions in French and waited patiently for their answers. And he was the strongest person they had ever met. Anika knew that when she got tired of walking, all she had to do was give his hand a tug and he would swing her up onto his shoulders.

Mara and Anika skipped on ahead. They loved the feel of their sundresses swishing against their legs and the way the warm air riffled over the bare skin on their arms and shoulders. Mara ran into the alfalfa field, put her wrists to-gether, and held out her hands like jaws. She closed them down quickly once, then again and again, trying to catch a grasshopper.

"I got one," she said at last and held out her arms. One hand was curved snugly over the other. When Anika came over, she moved her thumb a little and Anika peered in.

"Won't it pee green on you?" Anika asked.

"Only if it's scared."

"It's scared," Anika said. "It can't get out." She continued to look in. "What are you going to do to it?" When Mara didn't say anything, she said, "Don't hurt it." She remembered the boy at their school who had held up a housefly and started to pinch off one leg. He looked at Mara and Anika and their friends and asked, "Should I?" When the girls yelled "No!" he yanked the leg off. Then he asked again, and again they yelled "No!" One by one he pulled off its legs, and when he finished he held the legless fly between his finger and thumb and squeezed hard.

"I won't hurt it," Mara said. She ran over to Odine and opened her hands under Odine's chin. The grasshopper flew up at her neck. Odine shrieked and flapped her hands near her face. Mara and Anika giggled.

"Petite pest," Pierre said, and made as if to grab Mara, but she sprinted out of his reach and ran on ahead with Anika.

They were on the old wagon road, two well-worn, parallel dirt paths that cut through a farmer's field. Here and there alfalfa grew up the middle. The alfalfa went up under the girls' dresses and tickled their thighs. It feathered their bare arms. Every now and again Anika flicked the alfalfa from her skin.

Their father pointed out the old house on the rise in the wheat field and told Pierre and Odine about Willy the farmer, who sowed right up to the house. It was so old it didn't have any doors or windows, just the openings. Mara had been to the house once, with her father, and he'd told her to stay outside because some floorboards had rotted through. "It's no place for you to play. Stay there," he had said as he hoisted his leg over the window ledge and stepped inside. Then he bent his knees and put his weight down hard and bounced, as if he was riding a horse. The floorboards sagged a little under him, but they didn't give. He pulled himself up through the hole where the stairs used to be and a minute later called down to Mara through an upstairs window. Mara didn't want to look. She thought he would fall through the floorboards or out the window.

Further on, the road made its way down a long, steep hill toward the river. Willy didn't drive the tractor down that hill at all anymore; the road had slumped away near the bottom, and there were big chunks of upturned earth where the road used to be. Anika and Mara ran as fast as they could down the hill and jumped over the side of the tipped-up earth. The wall of roots and small stones poking through the dry grey soil was almost as high as Anika's head.

"Ow!" Anika said. She had caught a rose branch under her foot. Both girls were wearing plastic sandals that sometimes squeaked when they walked. Anika sat down, took off her sandal, and pulled out the thorn. Mara saw little tears in her eyes. Anika blinked hard, and the tears disappeared. "I'm okay," she said. This was Anika; she said she was okay even if she wasn't.

The sisters stopped in front of a clump of Saskatoon bushes and Mara pulled down a branch. They picked berries and ate until their fingers and lips were purply-red. Anika wiped her fingers on the back of her dress.

"Don't," Mara said, and pulled Anika's hand away. "Your new dress."

They walked along a narrow trail through some trees to the old field, the one Willy couldn't get to anymore. Some hay still grew there, all on its own. It was hard and, instead of tickling, it poked at them when they walked. It poked at their thighs and their arms, and so they pulled in their arms and sucked in their tummies and held their breath and stepped carefully through the hay.

When they got to the edge of the riverbank, they stopped and looked. They read the water the way they read words in a book. They watched it come from around a bend on their left and disappear around another bend on their right. Their eyes scanned the shoreline—the patches of grass, river willow, mud. Sandstone that periodically got washed away. The girls knew by the way the willow and the grasses stuck out of the dry mud and by how high the sandstones were that the river was low, even for late summer. Even so, they waited. They would not go near the water on their own.

Mara chased grasshoppers and caught one. In a minute the grown-ups arrived, laughing loudly about the things grown-ups laugh about. Mara moved close to Odine with her hands cupped in front of her stomach.

Pierre looked at her hands. "If that is another jumping creature, I will throw you into the river."

"No you won't," Mara cried.

"That was mean, Mara," her mother said. "No more grass-hoppers. Odine won't want to come back."

Mara looked at her mother in surprise. Odine was an old

friend of their mother's, from before university. She had always come back. As far as Mara knew, this was the first time she had come with anybody. Mara looked at Pierre for several seconds, and then opened her hands and let the grasshopper escape.

Their father made his way down the bank. After a few steps, he turned and reached out his hand to their mother, then handed the basket to her. Next he reached for Anika and held her up over his head. She spread out her arms and legs and cried, "Wheee!" He carried her down the slope, and she scrambled to the big sandstone where her mother had put down the basket and spread out a blue towel. Mara was too big; he couldn't lift her the same way, but he held her under the arms and swung her down.

It was Odine who helped Pierre.

"Pierre, my urban gentleman," Odine said to Mara's mother. Mara grinned, remembering how Odine had called Pierre a city boy after the mosquitoes had found them at the fire pit and he had jumped up and yelled "Merde!" and ran into the trees slapping his ears.

Mara and Anika had put their bathing suits on at the cabin. Now, they flipped their dresses over their heads, kicked off their sandals, and ran into the warm backwater upriver of the sandstone, splashing each other as they went. Their father came in, took the girls by the hand, and walked them up the river, staying close to the shore where the current was not so fast. Pierre ran after them, curious. He was curious about everything.

At the bend, the river was shallower and the water gabbled noisily over a gravel bar. Their father walked them along the gravel to the middle of the river, where the water only went up as far as their knees. Anika and Mara stood and watched while their father pulled a fat poplar log from the bank.

He held the log while the sisters grabbed on and slowly stepped off the gravel bar. The water gradually got deeper. First waist-deep and later, up to their necks. Mara and Anika floated on their bellies and kicked their legs, steering themselves back toward the little beach where they'd left their dresses. They saw their mother and Odine in the water, talking and laughing and sometimes looking over at them.

Pierre floated along beside them and reached for their ankles. They screeched and kicked hard and swam away. When they arrived at their beach, Mara and Anika hauled the log back up to the bend in the river. When they floated down again, they watched Pierre swim with Odine to the mud on the far shore just below the gravel bar. Their mother had told Odine about the place where there were no stones or grass or willows—just mud. Pierre slapped mud on Odine's breasts and her belly and between her legs. The echo of Odine's laugh bounced back at them from the other side of the river. Her bright yellow-and-orange bathing suit lay in the mud next to Pierre's blue swimming trunks.

The sisters hauled the log back up the river and walked off the gravel bar and floated down, over and over. Then they kicked their way to Pierre and Odine and dragged the log onto the shore. The only exposed parts of Pierre and Odine were their heads, hands, and feet. Anika tickled Odine's toes till Odine yelled, "All right, that's enough." Mara and Anika piled mud on themselves. Pierre reached over and spread mud in their hair.

"Hey!" Mara said. She scrambled out of the mud and pulled the log into the river. "Come on, Anika."

They floated down to their beach and squatted near the willow basket, hugging themselves and shivering. Water dripped off them and formed a dark ring in the sand around their bodies. Their mother came and wrapped them in towels.

"Here." She held out the basket of grapes and cookies and juice.

Mara chewed slowly around the edges of her cookie. Anika pulled out the tiny bits of chocolate and sucked them off her finger.

When they were warm again, Mara and Anika found clam shells to carve with in the soft sand. They made roads and houses, a store and a library. Mara took off her bathing suit and ran squealing into the water. Anika peeled off hers and ran in after her. They closed their eyes and dove under and came up with slicked-back hair. They were otters, Anika said. Seals, said Mara. She loved the feel of the water rushing over her naked skin and how light and fast she felt. In a few minutes the girls came out and returned to their sand village. After the sun dried them, they put on their sundresses and built more roads and more houses.

"I think there'll be a thunderstorm," their mother said.

Mara looked at the sky. It was blue. She didn't see a cloud anywhere. But she knew that sometimes, on very hot days, there were storms late in the afternoon.

"We have to go back and close the windows and start dinner."

"Can we stay?" Mara asked. "We know the way back."

Odine had floated down the river and now she sat on a rock near them. Their mother called out to her. There was no wind, and her voice was carried, high and clear, across the water. She said something in French. Odine called back in French and their mother laughed and said something else.

"Go on, have fun," Odine said.

"Make sure you listen to them," Mara's mother said, turning to Mara and Anika. "Don't run off or play little tricks."

She climbed up the bank with their father, and both of them waved at Mara and Anika and Odine.

"See you soon!" their father called.

Pierre swam up behind Odine and did something under the water that made her yell and laugh. Then she slapped him gently on the head, grabbed him, and pulled him under. Pierre slipped away and swam upstream. Mara watched. He swam hard, but after a minute he had only gone a short way. Then he floated back down, laughing, and gave his thick, wet hair a hard shake.

Pierre and Odine stepped out of the water, towelled themselves dry, and pulled on their clothes. They sat on a blanket watching the river and passing a cup of wine back and forth. Pierre pulled his camera from his cloth bag and took some pictures of Odine. Then he gestured toward the sisters, and Mara moved closer to Anika and smiled. *Click-click-click*, she heard. Bored, she turned back to the sand village. *Click-click*. She gathered sticks with Anika and poked them in the sand to make fences and lamp posts. After a time they found stones, long narrow stones the colour of milk chocolate, and slid them along the roads and parked them beside the houses and the school. They cupped their hands and scooped water to fill a small hole, the village swimming pool. Back and forth they went, from the river to the pool. Water leaked out of their hands and seeped into the sand, quicker than they could fill the hole, but they kept going. They knew the pool would never fill; this was how it was with these pools, and it was what they liked about them. In the back and forth they forgot where they were, what day it was, how long they had been there. That they would have to stop at some point. They became lost in this endless cycle from river to pool to river again. The entire world was still. The skin on Mara's shoulders pricked a little in the heat, but she didn't notice, not till later.

"Time to pack it up," Odine called suddenly.

"Aw," Anika and Mara said together. One voice rang out higher than the other, and the dissonant sound hung in the warm air briefly.

Mara saw that the light had changed. The sun was not so harsh and white. It was lower in the sky and orange.

"Will you come back with us tomorrow?" she asked.

"No, we are returning to the city tomorrow, and then home, remember? But we'll be back, you know that," Odine said. "You can't get rid of us."

Mara knew Odine would be back, but it had been so long since Odine last visited that she couldn't remember her. She remembered only the feeling of Odine being there. Anika didn't have any memory of Odine at all.

Pierre lifted Anika onto his shoulders and carried her up the riverbank. Then he came for Mara and did the same. She laughed out loud. "You're stronger than my dad," she said. "My dad can't lift me like this."

Pierre laughed too. He put her down and turned to give

his hand to Odine, but she had already bounded up the slope and was grinning at him.

They walked single file along the narrow path through the field, and after the slump at the bottom of the steep hill, Pierre lifted Anika onto his shoulders. Odine took Mara's hand. Mara's legs were tired, but she didn't say anything.

When they were near the old house, Pierre turned into the wheat field and said, "Let's make a detour." Mara followed, and Odine came last. The air crackled with the sound of the grasshoppers rubbing their wings. There weren't as many hopping now. Mara wondered if they got tired at the end of the day too.

Pierre walked around the old house. Mara and Anika stood near one corner, holding Odine's hands and leaning into her a little, basking in her warmth and in their own pleasant tired-ness. Pierre pulled out his camera and took pictures of the house. His camera had a long lens. He would look through the lens for several seconds before taking a picture. Sometimes he wouldn't take a picture at all but would pull the camera away from his face and walk on a few steps and look again.

Mara moved closer to the house. She peeked through a large window and sat on the ledge. The wood was grey and jagged and peeling. In some places it was rotting. Inside, she saw grass growing up through the gaps in the floor. Even a stalk of wheat. She swung her legs around to the inside and put her feet on the floor.

"Mara," Anika said, meaning, *Don't*.

Mara bent her knees the way her father had and bounced a few times without lifting her feet. The boards didn't break. They didn't even sag. She stood tall and looked around slowly. The house was not very large; the main floor was just one big room. Mara remembered Willy the farmer telling her parents that a family with ten children had lived here. She was itching to go upstairs but did not know how to get there.

She walked to the middle of the room. Her father's words buzzed in her head: "It's no place for you to play." She felt diz-zy. Outside, Pierre circled the house. He took pictures through the windows. There were four, one on each wall. He appeared and disappeared and appeared again. Mara thought of a horse in a carousel, going round and round. She listened for the sound of the wheat shaking to determine where he was. The next time he pointed his lens at her, she stuck out her tongue, and he pulled the camera away from his face and grinned in a way that said, "Okay, then," and moved away. When she saw him again he was taking a picture of Anika. Anika's face was turned into Odine's belly, and she peered back at him with only one eye.

Pierre went over and spoke to Odine, who looked down at Anika and said something to her. Anika shook her head.

"Mara," Odine called. "Pierre would like to take a picture of you and Anika, sitting in that window. The one you went through."

"Okay," Mara said.

Anika shook her head again.

"It's all right. Tell her it's all right, Mara," Odine said.

"Come on, Anika," Mara said. "Come sit in the window. Don't be such a baby. It's just a picture. Pierre likes to take pictures. Then we'll go back to the cabin and have dinner." Mara thought it was Pierre's job to take pictures, for a magazine probably.

The girls sat down side by side and looked out at Pierre. He asked them to sit with their backs against each other. Then he asked them to sit facing out with their heads close together. Then he wanted their backs up against the window frames and the soles of their plastic sandals touching.

Odine helped them sit just the right way. Sometimes she moved their hair a little. She said, "You girls are great. These will make great shots. We'll give copies to your parents."

Pierre nodded over at Odine, and she pulled off her clothes, stepped out of her sandals, and stood near the house, fully naked. Pierre looked through his lens. *Click-click-click* went the camera. Odine moved into the window ledge where the girls sat. Mara and Anika got up and picked stalks of wheat and pulled off the beards and the kernels.

"Mara," Odine said. "Anika. Come in the picture." She gestured with her hand to the ledge.

Mara knew what she meant. Odine meant for her and Anika to take off their clothes too. Mara giggled, though she thought it was more silly than funny. It would make a boring picture. But she pulled off her clothes and shoes anyway.

"Anika," Odine said. "You too."

Anika shook her head.

Pierre knelt down in front of her. "Just a picture. My camera doesn't bite." He put his hand into a crocodile jaw and made the jaw snap at her. Odine reached out quickly and pushed his hand away.

"Just like you were at the river," Odine said quietly. "Skinny-dipping."

"No it's not," Anika said in a high voice. "You can't skinny-dip without water." But there was Mara, sitting in the window ledge, just like Odine. Mara had left her pretty new dress in a clump beside her squeaky sandals.

Anika pulled off her dress and pink panties and came over and sat with her knees pulled close together against her chest and her clear eyes staring hard at the camera and her lips looking very small. She wanted to be back at the cabin, with her mother.

She thought of the way she had walked back and forth to fill the village pool that was never ever full, and how she had gotten so busy at it that she had forgotten where she was. She wanted to forget where she was again. She slid her hand along the window frame and felt a splinter dig into the palm of her hand. She blinked hard and turned to Pierre. *Click-click*, said his camera. *Click-click-click*. When there were a lot of clicks in a row, it sounded like the grasshoppers. Anika wondered if Mara needed to pee as much as she did. She didn't say anything, but she heard Mara breathing against her.

Then Pierre looked at Odine with a small smile on his face and put the lens cap back on. He was done.

Odine lifted Anika's dress over her shoulders for her. Anika didn't want help, but she didn't say anything. She didn't like the dress from Odine anymore. After Mara dressed, she felt the stinging on her shoulders and knew she'd been burned when she was making the village. She looked over at Anika's shoulders and saw that they were red too.

At the wagon road, Odine took Mara's and Anika's hands. Mara held on tightly. She wondered when Odine would come back, and if Pierre would come with her. She didn't want Pierre to come back, and she didn't want her sundress anymore. It was thin, so thin anybody could see her naked body right through it. And it made her feel cold, even though it was still warm out. What kind of dress was that, one you could see right through and that made you cold?

Anika moved her legs quickly to stay close to Odine. Pierre was walking slowly behind, and she hoped he would not catch up. Odine squeezed her hand harder and pushed the splinter farther into her palm, but Anika didn't feel it anymore. "I'm okay," she would have said, if anyone had asked. But nobody said anything. Everybody was too tired, or maybe no one had anything to say. No one, except the grasshoppers, which flew in the air around them, whispering *fleek-fleek*.

❧ THE GOLD ONE

Adele woke to the ringing of her cell phone. She grabbed the phone from the bedside table and flipped it open. "Hello," she said.

"Adele, it's Roxie. Sorry for the last minute, but I need to reschedule. Can you come in tomorrow instead of today?"

"No, Roxie." Adele looked at the clock radio beside her bed. Six in the morning. Six! It must be Wednesday. Roxie was Wednesdays.

"Okay, Friday, then," Roxie said. "Come in anytime on Friday."

"No. Not Friday either," Adele said.

"Can't you cancel someone?"

Adele laughed, a croaky morning laugh, though she didn't find it funny. She was good at that, though. She could laugh off pretty much anything. "No, I can't do that. You want me to do that to you?"

"Can you come in Saturday then? Bruno really wants the place nice for the weekend."

"Saturday's my day off. Sunday too. I have to have some days off, you know. I'll see you next Wednesday," Adele said firmly, and pushed the "off" button on the phone.

Now she had the morning off. Adele got up, humming, and started coffee. She put a slice of bread in the toaster and flipped through the *Woman's Day* magazine a client had given her. When the phone rang sometime later, she almost didn't answer. Then she glanced at the LCD screen and saw that it was old Henry Fitzwilliams. Henry was eighty-two and still lived on his own in that condo in the west end. He forgot to write things down sometimes. Or maybe it was just too hard for him.

"Adele?" It sounded like his throat was full of sandpaper. His voice was raspy and soft. "Adele?"

"I'm here, Henry."

"My daughter," he began, then took a breath, "My daughter is coming." He stopped again. He could be thinking or breathing. "To take me to tea." There was another pause. "This afternoon."

"Would you like me to come anyway, or wait till next week?"

"Next week." Pause. "Is fine." Adele waited. She saw that she'd torn the nail on her ring finger. "Wednesday?" Henry asked.

"Yes, I have you down for next Wednesday."

"Thank you, Adele."

"Bye-bye, Henry. Enjoy tea with your daughter."

She didn't mind about Henry. He didn't do it very often. It was Roxie who was getting to Adele. Roxie was picky like you wouldn't believe and she cancelled about once a month. Adele could put up with pretty much anything, but she didn't like to be treated like a doormat. Enough was enough.

The next morning she got up at four o'clock to drive her sister to the airport.

"You coulda given me more notice," Adele said after she'd settled herself into Jan's car.

"I just booked three days ago!" Jan said.

"Or maybe picked a later flight." Adele hated those last-minute hotel packages. They always came with an early flight, and she was the one taking Jan to the airport. "Where you off to this time?"

"Barbados."

"Good choice." Adele looked outside. There was a skiff of fresh snow on the road. Probably black ice too.

"Yup."

"You check the weather? I mean for hurricanes."

"Nah," Jan said. "I like to live dangerously. Is it even in the hurricane zone?"

"What, you're asking me?"

At the drop-off they both got out. Jan gave Adele a hug. "You're the best. Here's the key. It rides smooth. You'll see. It just purrs. You'll be getting one before you know it." She stroked the side. The gold Nissan shone, even in the dark.

"Right, in your dreams," Adele said. She could see her breath. "Get going. I'm freezing."

"Enjoy it while I'm gone!" Jan laughed. She pulled her suitcase through the airport's revolving doors.

Adele was nervous, driving home. She always drove Jan's car home so Jan wouldn't have to pay for parking, but Jan had never had a fancy new car like this one before. Adele drove slowly. People zoomed up behind, then shot past her. Sometimes they blasted their horns and glared. She didn't care.

The cell phone rang when she turned into her parking stall behind the apartment. She read the name on the screen: A M Stouge.

"Hello, Marnie," Adele said.

"Adele," Marnie said, "our son is in hospital down in Red Deer. We have to go down today and we won't be back till the weekend. Can we reschedule?"

Adele pulled her date book from her purse and leafed through it. "Next month, same day?"

"Sounds good. Oh, I have to go, Albert's calling."

Adele took a deep breath and paused before exhaling. Three cancellations in one week. It wasn't any week. It was the last week of the month. Rent was due. She would be short. She went inside and had a think. Then she dialled Roxie's number.

"Hello?" It was a young girl's voice. Roxie had a daughter, but she was all grown-up and at university somewhere.

"Oh, I think I called a wrong number. Is Roxie home?"

"Yes."

"Can I talk to her?"

"Yes."

Adele heard an adult voice, scolding, and then Roxie on the phone. "Hello? Hello?"

"It's Adele."

"Adele, oh. Sorry about that. We haven't talked to Zoe yet about answering the phone. She's only seven. We just got her last week. We're fostering her."

What next, Adele wondered. A while back she had been into training Seeing Eye dogs, but that only lasted a few months. Before that it was quilting. Adele saw a few squares of the quilt once, about two years ago, and hadn't seen hide nor hair of it since. Whatever. "I had a cancellation for today. Is today still good?"

"Oh, sorry, no. I made other plans."

Adele closed her eyes. "Saturday then? I can make it. Just this once." She was so annoyed with herself that she pinched her thigh. This is the problem, she thought, with being basically a nice person. I should just not go back at all.

"Saturday? Oh, yes. Eight o'clock?"

"I'll be there. Like I said, I don't work Saturdays—"

"I got that, Adele. Thank you." Roxie sounded genuinely pleased.

That night Adele stayed up for the ten o'clock news in case there was something about hurricanes. There was nothing about tsunamis or typhoons or even hurricanes anywhere on the entire planet. Well, Jan must be already in Haiti or Cuba or wherever she was off to by now, so nothing could be done about it if anything did happen. Adele dozed off and woke only when the news ended. She forced herself up off the couch and into bed. When she got there, she couldn't sleep. She lay in bed wide awake, going over and over in her mind how she'd tell Roxie she wasn't coming anymore. It should be easy. It should be so easy. They could find someone else, and Adele could fill their spot with another client. It was just that this week things were tight, but she'd find someone; she'd ask around. Why should she work for them? Boris was a filthy-rich, penny-pinching cheapskate. Things were worse now that he was semiretired and worked at home, in his den. Every week when it came time to pay he would move in close to Adele and say, "Let's pay you once a month, flat rate." And then he would tell her his flat rate. It was a good deal for him but a big cut for her. "Take a hike," she'd say, the way Roxie had taught her back when the two of them worked for the temp agency, the way that sounded funny and a little bit flirty but told someone you meant business. "I have to live too." Some days he got Roxie counting the minutes, and if Adele hadn't been there the full four hours, he got out his calculator and punched in numbers and pulled his earlobe or rubbed his fat nose and eventually came up with a figure and paid Adele less than her rate, down to the quarter sometimes.

She knew why she still worked for them. She still worked for them because they had been one of the first to hire her when she started up, when she really needed the income. They had helped her out when she really needed it. They gave her enough referrals to get herself on her feet. But she was doing fine now. She did not need their help anymore. The whole idea of this work was that she could be her own boss. For the first time ever, she worked for herself. It had taken a long time for her to get to this point. After she'd left the temp agency, she worked here and there and everywhere in retail, in a hotel chain, and for a time even had a sweet gig in a coffee shop—on everybody else's terms. She was not going back to that anymore, no way.

Saturday Adele got up early. Normally Saturdays were for sleeping in a little, sipping hot coffee from a real cup and even having a refill, and then calling a friend or going for a walk. When she had to take her coffee in a thermal mug, she usually forgot about it and it went cold. Well, today was the last time. She wouldn't spend all morning thinking about it; she wouldn't think about it at all, and when she left, she'd just tell Roxie she wasn't coming back. Just like that.

Adele took care of her things; she took her car in to the shop twice a year, and it ran well. But her car was nothing like Jan's new one. The Taurus was getting on. And the weather had turned, in the night. Jan had picked a good day to leave the city. They had said on the radio it was −24 with the wind chill. That kind of cold was hard on a car, even one that was looked after. Adele had a funny feeling in her stomach on the way to her car. She'd left it on the street because Jan's car, the nice one, was in her stall. But she knew, before she turned the key. She knew. Her car didn't start. No sound came. Nothing. Nada. Niente.

"Holy mother of God, the rent," she cried out and threw up her arms. Then she turned her head and saw Jan's Nissan. She didn't want to take it. She didn't even want to go near it. But Jan always let her use her car, and Adele was careful.

Adele pulled the buckets, rags, and cleaning solutions from her trunk and carried them to the Nissan. She was sweating a little, despite the cold. She drove so slowly she thought a cop would get her for not driving the speed limit. But not many people were out and about this early on a Saturday, not even the cops.

Roxie and Boris lived all the way out in the boondocks in a community called Courtney Heights, one of a zillion fancy schmancy subdivisions that had sprung up overnight. All of the houses looked the same. They all had double or triple front garages that barricaded the houses from the street. It was like nobody wanted to see what was happening outside or see who their neighbours were. Every house had a big picture window facing the front, with a room that never got used. A show room, with nice furniture, but people hardly sat in it. Siberia, Adele called that room.

When Adele drove past the sign announcing she was entering Courtney Heights, she thought, as she did every time she drove past the sign, that it was the strangest thing that Roxie's daughter was named Courtney. She would bet a day's pay the girl was named for Courtney Heights. But she would never ask. She could have asked back when she and Roxie worked together. It was the sort of thing they would have joked about at the Sherlock Holmes pub on a Friday night. It would have gone something like: I know a lady with a kid named Courtney and she lives in Courtney Heights. And they both would have cracked up, let it rip till they had tears coming and their sides hurt, like they did about the lady boss they had named Candy.

They couldn't believe a grown-up woman boss would let herself be called Candy. They called her Eye Candy the first time they saw her, but then she spoke to them and she was Drill Sergeant from that moment forward, DS for short. Even the men were different around her. Adele thought it was strange. Nobody laughed near DS; they were too terrified. But at the Sherlock Holmes, later, Adele and Roxie would have a good laugh about her names, the one she went by and the one they called her, and they would have a lot to say about her, too. Her and Young Buck and Tom Cat. Now, though, Adele didn't say anything to Roxie about Courtney Heights or about Boris. She knew what to say and what to laugh about when she cleaned people's homes.

When Adele rang the bell, Roxie answered. She was wearing a blue velour housecoat with matching slippers, and she held a mug of coffee in her hands. Adele wondered where she'd left hers. Maybe in the car. More likely on the kitchen counter. Probably it already had a milk skin on top and was stone cold.

"Thank you for coming today," Roxie said. A wisp of a girl came up behind her. Roxie turned to her. "This is Zoe."

Zoe looked up at Adele and then scooted up the stairs.

"Oh, you're welcome, Roxie," Adele said, smiling at her.

Adele started in the main floor bathroom and worked her way through to the kitchen at the back of the house. Roxie was at the stove when Adele got there. She was dressed now.

"Just leave the dishes," Roxie said. "I'll take care of them." As Roxie pulled rubber gloves over her fingers, Adele noticed how fine her hands looked. Adele's were always rough and dry. She didn't have back problems though. Four years of cleaning homes had kept her fit. She might change careers again, but not yet.

Roxie's eyes fell over Adele's face. "It's so nice having you here," she said. "You're always humming. It really cheers the place up."

"Oh, I like to hum," Adele said. "It's how I work. It just goes easier." She had thought she'd feel much happier than usual,

knowing it was her last day here, but she knew she was waiting till the drive home. Then she'd let loose.

They heard the hall door to the garage open and close.
"That's Boris, off to the store with Zoe," Roxie said. "They're
probably getting a video for tonight."

"She looks like a sweet girl," Adele said.

Roxie didn't say anything.

Adele finished the counters and started on the floor.

"We've heard different things about fostering children,"
Roxie said. "She's young enough that she hasn't been into
any serious trouble. We'll see how she works out. Boris wasn't
all that keen on her." She stared out the window and then said,
"But I wanted someone. Courtney's gone, you know. Boris is
plugged into the computer all day." She watched Adele. "You
ever find it too quiet, on your own? No, I guess you wouldn't,
you can just sing, you're so happy."

"My dear," Adele said, not pausing in her countertop wiping,
"I have enough work and enough friends. I have enough. It's
not too quiet." Inside, she paused, though. This was as much
of a peek into her world as Roxie had ever allowed.

"Do you think much about those days we were temping?"
Roxie asked.

"Now and then." Adele wondered where Roxie was going
with that question. She hadn't asked before. Adele had wondered, when she first started cleaning for her, if it would even
come up.

Roxie looked at the door to the garage and then at Adele.
"Boris liked you, didn't he," she said. "Way back, I mean. When
we were temping." She turned away quickly.

The way Roxie said it, in bits and pieces, and then looked
the other way, made Adele feel that Roxie had wanted to say
this for a long time. She glanced over at Roxie's back and her
rounded, slumping shoulders, the left one a little lower than
the right one. "Oh no. Oh no. He always liked you."

Adele was not good at lying. She began to sing "When I
was just a little girl" and made her way out of the kitchen
and upstairs. She didn't tidy or make beds; she washed floors

and vacuumed and dusted. She did the main bathroom first
and the little girl's room next. The door to Courtney's room
was always closed, and Roxie had said not to bother going
in there. Adele always did the master bedroom last. She put
it off in case something came up and she didn't have to go
into it. That had never happened, but the thought was always
at the back of her mind. It was strange to see Roxie's flimsy
nightie or maybe a lacy black bra and Boris's slightly smelly
underwear tossed carelessly onto the bed. When she got to
the photograph of Boris and Roxie on the dresser, their wedding shot, she picked it up and wiped slowly and looked. Boris
had that same half smile he had now, that same piercing look
that had held her the first time he had caught her eye. And
Roxie. Well. Look at that face. Young and beautiful and happy.
So happy. Like that day was the culmination of everything.
Like she was finally where she wanted to be. Adele wondered
how soon reality had set in.

They had to dress up for temping work, not like now—
these days Adele wore old jeans or sweat pants and a T-shirt.
Back then she had to wear short, tight skirts every day and high
heels and so much makeup, not just a wisp here and there—
she had to really apply it. It took an hour just to get ready.
Adele went through so many pairs of pantyhose in those days.
They went from job to job, Adele and Roxie, sometimes to the
same office, sometimes not, but they were never far apart. At
every job there was always a guy, maybe the boss, who would
stare at Adele when she walked away from his desk, stare at
her behind. Or stare at her front for way too long. Adele had
a figure then. Roxie did too, but Roxie was smart, about the
men, anyway. Adele tried hard to be like her, because Roxie
knew so much and had a look like she knew what she wanted.
At the Sherlock Holmes on Fridays, where Roland the bar-
tender would pour their gin and tonics before they even sat
down, Roxie would tell her how to catch the men looking and
how to glance at them with your eyes so they knew, and what
to say to the men before you slipped away. How to pretend
like it was all fun so the men would keep it easy and not get

put off by you because that could change everything. If you didn't know how to laugh with them in the right way or look at them in the right way they might think you were stuck-up and not even talk to you, and the days would be unbearably long and you might end up in some dive or get the work nobody wanted. So Adele watched Roxie and learned pretty quickly how to look and when to laugh.

They met Boris at one of the temp jobs. He was a manager at one of the companies that called them in, mainly to do a lot of filing that had backed up. He came on to Adele first, that was how it happened. He came on to her first, and there was something about him she liked, something about the way he looked at her that made her weak in the knees and gave her a tingling feeling in the chest that left her giddy. They even made out a few times. Some far-off instinct told her to keep it to herself, to not let Roxie in on it. Then he started to talk like he was her boss even when they weren't in the office. She was not having any of that so she called it off, and for a week or so she had second thoughts; maybe he wasn't so bad? Even her parents, back home in St. Paul, practically on another planet, would be mad that she had turned down someone with such a good job. But he was already onto Roxie by then, and everything happened fast from that point. One minute he was asking Roxie out and the next they were getting married and Roxie was gone. Adele didn't know till then that that was the only reason Roxie had been working temp all along: for a way out and a way in.

As soon as Roxie got married, she had the baby girl and was too busy for anything, even to call Adele. Every Friday on the way to the Sherlock Holmes with one of the other temps, Mary Ann or Brenda or whoever, Adele thought about calling her, but she knew Roxie would be too busy now for drinks. When the girl was old enough to be in school, Adele thought maybe Roxie could go out, but so much time had passed that Adele didn't know what she'd say to her. It was Boris who called, completely out of the blue. Right when she was starting up on her own four years ago. All those years had passed, but his voice sounded just like it had yesterday. She should have said no right off, but there he was, telling her about Roxie's bad back and how they used to have so much fun together, and before she knew it she was saying yes.

Adele set the wedding photo back on the dresser, finished cleaning the bedroom and the ensuite bathroom, and made her way down to the den off the kitchen. Boris was there. He'd been there a long time—she had heard him come in when she was cleaning the upstairs bathroom. He sat on a black swivel chair in front of his computer, staring and clicking. She hummed happily to herself, and even began to sing. She sang the songs her mother used to sing, "Que Sera, Sera" and "Non, je ne regrette rien," and hoped he wouldn't turn and look at her.

When Adele moved to the living room, Zoe flitted in on her tiptoes and looked up at her. Adele smiled over at her.

"Can you sing that one again?" Zoe asked.

"Which one?"

"About when you were a little girl and you asked your mother if you would be pretty."

Adele smiled again. "You like that one?"

Zoe nodded.

Adele sang the first verse. When she finished, she asked, "Did you pick out a video?"

Zoe stared at her and then skittered off. Adele carried on dusting. She liked the children in all the homes she cleaned, and usually they came to see her and talk to her. They wanted to know what she was doing and how she did it, and then they would ask if they could try dusting or vacuuming. She always let them.

When Adele was done she gathered her buckets and put them by the door. She felt tired all of a sudden. "I'm heading out!" she called. Roxie came down the stairs, and Boris trotted in from the den.

"Adele," he said, "what about our flat rate deal? We pay you once a month, flat rate. Easier all around. How about it?"

"Forget it," Adele said. "I have to live too, you know." There was nothing nice about the way she said it.

He looked at Roxie, and Adele knew he wanted her to say how long Adele had been there—had it been three hours and forty-eight minutes, three hours and fifty-two minutes?—but Roxie didn't say anything. He shoved a wad of bills at Adele, the right amount. She saw when she discretely checked before tucking it into her jeans pocket. Then she grabbed the bucket and cleaning supplies and went outside. There he went again, trying to swindle her! It made her so mad she didn't think to tell Roxie she wasn't coming anymore till she was halfway down the steps. But she knew Roxie. Roxie would beg and plead and try to get her to stay, and Adele was not up for that. She just wanted to be home. She'd leave Roxie a message later. Tonight, she was going to celebrate. Maybe a glass of wine, maybe call Claude, who had been interested in her for some time, to see if he was up for a movie.

"Oh, Lord," she said when she got to the street. Her Taurus was gone. "Oh, Lord." Then she remembered that she had taken Jan's car, and she laughed at herself for being so out of it. There was Jan's car, right where she'd left it. She put the cleaning supplies in the trunk and went to unlock the door, and it was only then she saw the dent by the headlight on the driver's side. She knelt in front of the Nissan. It was a huge dent. There were bits of the headlight cover on the road.

Adele picked up the yellow and red plastic pieces and walked back to the house and opened the door. Roxie and Boris were still in the front hall. He was saying something to her and she was shaking her head. They turned to her in surprise.

"Did you forget something?" Roxie asked. Sometimes Adele forgot a rag, but she didn't worry about that.

"My car! Did you see my car? It's not even my car, it's my sister's. Brand new." She held out the pieces of broken plastic.

"What?" Roxie slipped on her shoes and walked down the sidewalk to the street. Adele was right behind her. "Oh my God!" Roxie said when she saw the dent. "Who would do that? That's awful. Hit and run, too. Come inside and call the police." She pulled her sweater tightly around her front.

"Oh, I wouldn't bother." Boris was behind Roxie. "Look—" he glanced up and down the street, his hands turned palms upward and empty at the hopelessness of it all—"you'll never find who it was. Just go in and file a report. Your insurance will cover it."

"It's my sister's new car!" Adele wailed. She started walking along the street, searching for the driver who had hit her car and seeing countless long tire marks in the fresh snow. She held the broken pieces against her belly and felt sick to her stomach.

"Come," Roxie said. She took Adele's arm lightly and led her inside and back to the kitchen. "Here," she said and handed Adele the phone. She opened the phone book and started reading out the numbers.

Adele dialled slowly. After one ring a smooth female voice said, "Police station, please hold."

She slumped against the table. She was hot in her coat but didn't take it off. The other end of the line was so quiet she wondered if she'd been cut off. In the silence she began speaking to her sister, softly. "Oh, Jan. I'm so sorry, Jan. Oh my Lord it will cost a fortune..." Soon she realized she was talking louder to hear herself over the noise coming from the den. At first it was just background voices, but after a minute Adele knew it was an argument. Boris's voice came through the loudest.

"How can you trust her?" he was shouting. Then Roxie's voice, high-pitched, but not so loud. Adele couldn't make out what she was saying.

"She's a child!" It was Boris again. The walls shook. "We don't know anything about her."

Zoe, the slip of Zoe, came into the kitchen. Her face was soft and full of worry.

Adele was so alarmed by the child's distress that she put the phone on the table and knelt in front of her and said, "Don't cry. Don't be afraid." The fight was getting louder and had a meanness to it that made Adele feel sick. She felt sick in her stomach and her chest and even her bones; she was filled with the sense that something bad was going to happen and whatever it was it didn't concern her and she should leave quickly, but she could not bring herself to leave the girl behind. "They'll stop soon," she said, though she didn't believe it. The argument was becoming more intense.

"You can't be serious!" Boris shouted, and the walls shook. "She could be lying. You don't know what these kids are like, Roxie."

"We didn't get a video," Zoe said.

"How about a hundred bucks?" Boris bellowed. "A hundred bucks and be done with it."

"What? What did you say? A video?" The shouting was so loud Adele could barely hear herself, but she thought if she kept talking, she could distract the girl. "Oh, you'll get one another time. Don't worry. Maybe you'll watch the television tonight instead, eh? Is that why you're sad?"

Zoe shook her head. "We didn't get it because he scrunched the car so we had to come right back."

"If I were in her shoes, I'd be happy to take a hundred bucks!" Boris yelled.

"Who scrunched the car?" Adele asked. "What car?" Though she knew and felt sicker still.

The girl didn't say anything. Their faces were so close that Adele felt the girl's breath. Zoe's eyes darted across Adele's face.

"Zoe. Tell me. Who?"

"Him." She pointed to the den. "The dad."

"What car, Zoe?" Adele asked. She knew that, too, but she wanted to hear Zoe say it.

"The shiny gold one out front. The pretty one. After the scrunch he put his big car right back in the garage so no one would see. I told the mom that. When you were upstairs." She chewed her lower lip for a few seconds. "It's your car, isn't it?"

"My sister's. My sister Jan's." *How on earth am I going to tell Jan,* Adele thought. "It's okay," she said, though nothing about it was okay. "It's not your fault." *Maybe if I sing to Zoe, I can block out the shouts. Maybe the shouting will end soon and I can go home.* "You want me to sing?"

"I'll have to leave again," Zoe said. Her small face was pinched.

"What?"

"Whenever there's yelling, I have to leave." She stared at Adele with small, hard eyes.

❧ GIVING BLOOD

On a Monday night, I went for dinner at Earls, a restaurant where parrots perch overhead and luscious green palms surround the tables, creating the illusion of holiday beaches and blue cloudless skies and heat. Mr. Richards asked for a spinach salad, with extra almonds. I ordered a BLT sandwich. Mr. Richards and I ate quickly. We hurried. We were late. It was nearly seven o'clock, and at seven I would begin telephoning Red Cross blood donors: I was a telephone volunteer.

Every Monday night at seven I sat in at a desk inside a V-shaped nook and spoke into a piece of cream-coloured plastic and asked strangers for their blood. I sat in a small room with three other volunteers from Mr. Richards's high school chemistry class. I jammed the telephone tightly between my ear and my shoulder. My hands were free to book appointments and leaf through pages and pages of blood donors' telephone numbers and draw spindly trees and wide-petalled flowers in the margins. The next day, the next week, though I held my head upright and stood tall, I felt the crick in my neck and that hard plastic jammed unnaturally against my ear.

The first time we came Mr. Richards had driven us to the Red Cross building in his dark green Buick. He unlocked the back door of the building and took us on a tour.

"The donors," he explained, smiling, "go in the main door and check in *here*." He gestured toward a brown book. Except for this first evening, Mr. Richards usually said very little. Instead, he pointed, gestured with his hands, moved his head or eyes. "Always identify yourself when you come here during the day. Always let people know who you are. And what your intentions are." He paused. "If you drive a Porsche, for instance, make sure you let people know so you get faster service." He waited for us to get his joke. I looked at the others and we giggled uncertainly. We were in the eleventh grade. None of us had a car.

Mr. Richards was a tall man. He was about fifty years old, I guessed, and starting to lose hair from the top of his head. He spoke quietly, so we had to stand close and strain to listen. He listened with the same focussed attention when his students had something to say. We all talked to him. About everything. He smiled warmly at us. His blue eyes were bright. He was a happy man.

We followed Mr. Richards past the donor beds, the rest area, and the plasmapheresis beds with their tiny television sets attached to long mechanical arms. He showed us his Volunteer Co-ordinator of the Year award in the Volunteer Hall of Fame. He had the same plaque at home, he said. "This is how they thank you, when you bring in so much fresh blood." He smiled, and we smiled too, because we thought we should. We stopped at the donor-volunteer coffee corner, where cookies and soft drinks had been left out for us. At this time of night, the blood machines were shut down and the beds were empty. Not a soul was in sight.

"Help yourselves," Mr. Richards said. He nodded toward the Voortman cookies and poured himself coffee in a Styrofoam cup.

I never liked the taste of Voortman cookies.

"Always be polite," Mr. Richards reminded us the first night. "Never push. Joke if you're comfortable. Tell them"—he paused, letting the words come slowly—"you're a vampire. You want to suck their blood. That usually relaxes them." His lips widened into a big smile, and we laughed.

Mr. Richards didn't telephone blood donors. He sat, ready to answer our questions and to deal with difficult calls, at his desk on the other side of our soundproof room, watching us through the glass wall. I didn't like this arrangement. I told myself, every Monday night, that he didn't like it either. He couldn't possibly. He told me, when I asked, that the glass was there because there were too many distractions during the day. The daytime telephone volunteers couldn't do their jobs. I pictured the daytime women, before the glass was there, sitting with their backs to the room and feeling light flutterings against their ears and necks.

We knew from the tour where people gave blood, where we could have a cookie break, and where we worked. Everything had a place.

But the building is very large. There are other rooms.

Six o'clock one Monday night. Mr. Richards took Lisa and me for dinner at Earls, a restaurant where blue and red parrots hang from the ceiling and monstrous green palms surround the tables.

Lisa and I had done some extra volunteer work on the weekend. We'd been hostesses at a satellite donor clinic at Castledowns Mall. And now, Mr. Richards was taking us out for dinner. The two of us. It was a real treat, because we didn't go out to dinner with our families. My kid brother threw food off his plate when he didn't like it. He screamed in public places. He hadn't learned how to sit still until the adults were finished. Lisa and I ordered burgers with fries and talked about telephoning. My fingers reached up to my neck.

"Some of them don't find it funny," I said. "When I ask for their blood."

"It's how you say it," Lisa said.

"Remember, you're doing a good thing," Mr. Richards said. "Supporting a good cause."

"Sometimes they tell me not to call back," I said. "They hang up on me. I want to hang up on them."

Lisa and I liked talking to Mr. Richards. We told him what we wanted to do on the weekend. We told him what we wanted to be when we grew up.

"You never know," Mr. Richards said, smiling. "One day, one of you might be a nurse and take people's blood."

"Yuck!" Lisa and I said one breath.

The parrots squawked. The palms swayed gently in the breezes. A black one with teeth darted through the leaves. We were quite sure, later, Lisa and I, that we were somewhere warm. Somewhere faraway. Somewhere *else*.

"So, how do you like being vampires?" Mr. Richards asked.

Lisa laughed and said, "It's fun."

She didn't actually come. Mr. Richards and I sat down at a table for two.

There is, of course, a room at the back where the cookies are stored.

Six o'clock one Monday night, Mr. Richards and I went for dinner at Earls, where colourful parrots mimic curious words, where a breeze from a fan brushes a frond against a bruised neck.

I ordered a BLT sandwich. Mr. Richards ordered a spinach salad with extra almonds. We talked about math class, about English essays, about my younger brother. Was I getting anything out of volunteering? Yes, I said, yes, and moved my fingers self-consciously to my neck. The bruise must be so red and large now that everybody could see.

And will my summer job interfere with my volunteering? he wanted to know. His voice was gentle, but the words came hard and quick, chop chop chop. I stopped chewing and looked over at him. I shook my head. His blue eyes wandered lazily across my face. They looked sad. It was a strange sadness, because he was so happy.

"There's something you're not telling me," he said. My mouth opened to speak, but he was quicker. "You've always told me everything," he said, and I knew by the way he said it that I hadn't—of course I hadn't. "Talk to me," he whispered. The space was silent now except for his breathing, his slow and forceful breathing. His eyes were deep and sunken, as if he hadn't slept for days. His eyes said, If you just talk to me, everything will be all right again.

Voortman cookies are hard and dry.

My BLT was so thick a toothpick held it together.

"What do you mean?" I said. I was exasperated. He was sad and I didn't know what I was supposed to do about it.

"Just anything. Tell me anything," he invited. His voice was low. I almost didn't hear it.

I started to laugh, then choked on a piece of bacon. I looked at his soft, quiet face to see if he was joking. He was smiling again. His eyes had a light in them. But he wasn't joking.

"You know I take an active interest in my students," he went on. "In young people." His voice was almost inaudible now, but it seemed to me that the couple at the next table could hear him through the palms, that even the couple beyond them could hear. I stared at the farther couple, wondering what sounds were coming from the jaunty, animated movements of their lips. What was he saying, way over there, and was she so far away that it wouldn't come to her till later, much later?

"Go on then," Mr. Richards continued.

The room at the back is not a huge room. It's more like a closet. On the wall are six shelves of cookies, from the floor to the ceiling. Count them. You love cookies. Six shelves. There are boxes and boxes of Voortman cookies. Chocolate chip. Oatmeal. Raisin. Sugar. Shortbread. Peanut butter. Almond. They are packed loosely in big boxes, so as soon as you open a box, you can reach in and take a cookie.

A BLT is a toasted sandwich, and at Earls that Monday night the toaster made the bread so crisp and dry it grated at the inside of my mouth. The bacon was practically raw.

"Well?" He breathed deeply as he waited.

Bastard, I thought. The thought was so far in the back of my head I didn't hear it, not then. But the parrots heard it. They picked it up and tossed it from one to the other, croaking it again and again, their hoarse cries sliding down the broad leaves of the palms and gliding up again. They repeated it in different ways, louder and softer, faster and slower, like small children who have just learned a new word and share it with everyone they meet. And there, in the corner on the ceiling, in the dark, a black parrot, upside down, its sharp teeth barely visible. Not a parrot. Not a parrot at all. I sat unable to move, watching for the server to arrive with the bill, watching Mr. Richards eat his salad, staring down at the mess of bacon and lettuce in a pool of red tomato juice. And everywhere, crumbs. How would the server ever clean this mess?

I waited to go, to return to my seat behind the soundproof glass, to begin to breathe again, my own breath, just my own.

Voortman cookies leave a vile aftertaste on your tongue.

Six o'clock one Monday night. Mr. Richards and I went for dinner where parrots hang from the ceiling and palm trees surround the diners. We ate quickly so we wouldn't be late for telephoning. We ate so quickly we didn't have a chance to speak at all, which was just as well as I could hardly breathe. Mr. Richards wrapped his hands around a clubhouse sandwich, large heavy hands that were warm, warm like the tropical sun, and we had so little time he didn't say anything at all, but his lips didn't stop moving, not once.

That wasn't true of course. Even the parrots will tell you he ate a spinach salad that day.

The night we ran out of cookies, I stood on the top of the stepladder and he stood behind. To steady the ladder, he said. It wobbled, he said. When I felt the wings against my legs, heavy, fluttering wings, the sound leapt out on its own, a parrot's hoarse squawk, an involuntary cry from my throat, with nowhere to go in that small space. First flapping wings, then beaks nestling, claws snatching. I leapt up and grabbed the boxes. They fell, first one, then another, still more, breaking open, the cookies tumbling out over my head. Hands flew up to stop them. Reaching for the cookies, he said later. Such a confusion, he said. The wings sent a shiver along my back while cookies continued to fall like maimed birds—dry, brute things unable to save themselves as they plunged.

That night we went to Earls, Mr. Richards moved too slowly. His mouth formed words I almost couldn't hear.

"Come now," he prodded. "You can tell me."

The dinner was intended to make up for spilling all the cookies. So I wouldn't feel bad about breaking so many cookies, he said. Because it was an accident.

"You *are* enjoying yourself, I hope." His eyes narrowed slightly as he waited for me to respond. I looked away and saw the farther couple again. The man's mouth continued to form words, an endless stream of words I could not make out, while the woman rose up and floated away between the swaying palms.

"You are getting something out of volunteering," he continued.

When bacon is half raw, white, thick, it gets stuck in your throat and on your tongue and sits there so you can barely speak. Mayonnaise, stained pink from tomato juice and soft, runs down your hands and sometimes you don't have a napkin to wipe on. Your hands are red now too, red from the dripping tomato. You think about wiping your hands on your jeans, but that would leave a stain.

"Aren't you?" he asked.

When bacon turns cold and the toast crumbles, a BLT is not an appealing dinner.

"These things," he went on, "are important."

I moved my head to one side and felt a throbbing in my neck. When you are having trouble breathing, you want to save your breath, so you don't speak at all.

"We have to hurry," he reminded me. Then, glancing down at the mess of bacon and lettuce and tomato and toast, he added, "My treat."

🦋 BUTTERFLIES

He's sitting on the top of a ladder under the branches of the red apple tree, picking apples and setting them in a pouch that's wrapped around his belly. Nobody's ever been to our farm before. Nobody ever comes. We boys get up to no good when people come. That's why Mom moved us out here.

"Who are you?" I holler.

"Hello there," the man says. "I'm Henry."

"What are you doing up there?"

"I'm picking apples."

"You allowed to do that?"

The man smiles widely and then laughs. I like his laugh. "Your dad asked me to," he says. "Here"—he climbs down the ladder and hands me an apple. His eyes are blue and kind and he has rough, scratchy fingers with dirt under the nails. "You must be Oliver," he says.

"Yep."

"Here, Oliver, see all those bruised apples on the ground? They go in the blue bucket. For the horses. These good ones go in the red bucket. Go on."

I fill up the blue bucket, and there are still a hundred apples on the ground. Mom calls me to come in then. She pushes away the house-fixing books she has spread out on the kitchen table and puts a peanut butter and jam sandwich at my place.

Mom sits beside me and listens while I read about boring old Frog and Toad. Then she starts dinner, and after a while Dad comes home. He gives her a kiss and goes to the big bedroom to change out of his fancy work clothes, his shiny shoes and nice white shirt and the jacket that matches his pants, and put on his home clothes—jeans and a wrinkly green shirt that smell like Dad. He comes up to Mom, takes her cheeks in both hands and says, "You like it yet, Ellie? Apple trees, a stable, fields, a huge forest. All this space. Just us and a bunch of dumb coyotes." He laughs loudly and then grabs a handful of peanuts from the bag on the counter and says, "Oh, I've hired Henry's daughter."

"Who?" Mom asks.

"Henry's daughter. Leta," Dad says. He leans against the counter.

"Why?" Mom yells. I don't know if she's mad or just yelling because her head is in the fridge.

"What do you mean, *why?*" Dad says, and tosses a few peanuts into his mouth.

"Just that," Mom says. "Why?" She closes the fridge and puts a jug of milk on the table.

"To help with the horses," Dad says. "We talked about it. You said hire someone. I hired someone. Leta's starting tomorrow. She'll come in when she's not in classes at the college. Anyway, Henry will drive her."

Mom makes a frowny face. Then she looks at me and says, "Oliver, go wash up. Benny!" she calls down the stairs. "Dinner!"

Benny leaps up the stairs two at a time and swings me up onto his shoulders. He puts me down in the bathroom.

"After you, Blue," Benny says, and yanks my ear. I kick backward and get him in the shin. It hurts my heel but I don't cry. I never cry. Mom's the only one who cries.

We race to the kitchen and crash into our chairs.

"Child!" Mom yells. She plops cheesy noodles onto my plate beside some peas and meat.

"Oliver, you want to come feed the horses after dinner?" Dad asks.

"Yup."

"Don't talk with your mouth full," Mom says. "Finish your pork chop," she says. But she's smiling. She likes that Dad has horses like when he was a kid and she likes that we feed them together. Most of the time, though, she's not smiling because we boys are getting into trouble and causing her grief.

"Hey, Mom, Dad," Benny says, "you gotta go to Matthew's."

"Who's Matthew?" Dad asks.

"Matthew Wiley, in my class," Benny says. "He lives two fields over. You gotta go."

"What's at the Wileys'?" I ask. "Can I go?"

"Mr. and Mrs. Wiley had a big fight last week," Benny says, "and Mr. Wiley got up and drove off. He hasn't come back. He left his dinner on the table, and the dinner's still there. Steak and baked puddadahs and green beans. It's gross. And Mrs. Wiley's been sitting at her kitchen table for days drinking wine till her head falls off. I told you I didn't want to move out here. I told you it was a bad idea. You gotta check it out, Mom. Matthew hasn't had anything to eat for days. Mrs. Wiley's forgot how to cook—"

"Stop screaming, Oliver," Mom yells, and pulls me onto her lap. She squeezes my head against her chest so hard I can't breathe. "Benny, don't do that again," she says. "And you," she says to me, "settle down, it's all right."

"Her head fell off!" I squeak from under Mom's arm. "And Matthew isn't getting anything to eat!"

"Ha!" Benny snorts. "You're so gullible."

"Come and feed the horses," Dad says, and takes my hand. His is warm and big, and he holds on tight. I run to keep up. He stares down at the gravel with the squinty-frowny look he has whenever he takes off. Sometimes he just takes off, in his head, and I don't say anything till he's back because I know he won't hear it.

We give the pony Anthony some grain and then feed Prince and Chuck. I find two apples in the bruised apple bucket and hold them out to Prince. Dad told me the horses he had when he was a boy had the same names.

"Dad," I say. "Are you glad we moved here?"

Dad lifts me up and has a think. "Do *you* like it here?" he asks. I nod, and he gives me Chuck's brush. I smell Dad's clean smell and the smell of fresh straw mixed with pooped-in straw and Chuck's dusty smell, and soon Dad gets a horse-stall smell too. I like that smell on him. It's Dad's home smell. I don't like his city smell. I don't think Mom does either. She smells his city shirts sometimes after he takes them off. She holds them right against her face and smells and smells. Not with a smiling face, like the mothers on television showing us how clean they make their husbands' shirts. Mom looks mad when she smells his shirts. I asked her once if she liked his city smell and she looked at me and said, "What are you doing in here?" and shoved me out of the bedroom.

Dad talks to Chuck about me brushing him and how shiny his coat is getting. He says it like Chuck understands everything. After a while he says, "I'll tell you something about horses, son. They never talk back. They're happy to see you and don't complain about the feed. They don't care where you've been or ask when they'll see you again. It's a strange world, Oliver. A woman never forgets one dumb thing a man did, no matter how many smart things he does to make up for it, and men, well, we're just around to make trouble for women. A horse might be your best friend one day."

When I get home from school the next day, there's a girl in the stable.

"Henry," I yell. Henry's up the ladder in the yellow apple tree. He rubs an apple on his shirt front and hands it down to me. "Henry," I say again, "there's someone with Chuck. That your girl?"

"That's my Leta," Henry says.

I run over to the stable. Leta's tall, even taller than Benny. Her face is up to Chuck's cheek. She has hair the colour of shiny straw that goes halfway down her back. She doesn't have pimples like Benny, and she doesn't have soft parts like Mom. Her big black rubber boots go all the way up her shins and her jeans have rips in the knees and her shirt's too long. She smooches Chuck's cheek, brushes him, and smooches some more. Then she stops and turns to me. She has kind eyes, like Henry.

"Hello," she says. "Who are you?"

"I'm Oliver, the little brother. You know why we call our farm Foulstone Creek Farm?"

"Uh, no, how come?"

"Because Foulstone Creek runs right through it!" I say. Leta laughs. I want to say something else funny, but I'm not the funny one in our family. That's Dad. "Will you hitch the pony up to the cart?"

"You have a pony and a cart?"

"Yep, Anthony. My dad lets Benny and me take it out," I say. "If we're careful."

Benny only took me once and said he would never go again. He said it was dumb, riding a piece of junk on wheels and having people gawk at us and take our picture. When the people got their cameras out, he shouted at them to take a hike and shook the reins to make Anthony go faster. It's not a piece of junk. Dad bought it when we came here so we could do fun things, all four of us. He said Mom won't go on a horse but she'd go in the cart maybe. Except whenever Dad asks her to come she says, "Not today, boys."

"We can ride to the Shell station on the highway and get candy," I tell Leta.

Mom calls me in for my snack. I dump my coat and shoes and backpack by the door. But not my apple.

"Is that from Henry?" Mom asks.

"Yep."

"He's a nice man," Mom says, and then: "I hope it works out with Leta. As long as she's responsible and gets the work done. Here," she says. She puts a peanut butter sandwich on the table and sits next to me and listens to me read about Horrible Harry.

Mom is happy with Henry, and I know she's happy with Leta, too, because Leta's there the next day. I get off the school bus and run down our lane to the stable and watch her take Prince's saddle off. His belly is shiny and wet and steam comes off it.

"Hi, Sport," Leta says. "Here, help me hang this saddle."

She's done her work now so we go round behind the stable. Nobody can see us back here. We sit on the mound and make pictures in the dirt with sticks. Leta makes a smiley face. I make one too. Leta makes two up-and-down lines and two side-to-side lines and an X in the middle.

"Your turn," she says. "Make an O."

"I know this game," I say, and make an O.

X, O, X, O.

"You win," Leta says. She draws a line through the three Os. I know she let me win. "Look," she says, and makes three small Xs and three small Os, all in a line. "Means hugs and kisses," she says.

"I know that," I say and give her a hug and a kiss.

Leta laughs. Her face is even prettier when she laughs. Then she says, "I bet you love it here. It must be great to have all this space to run wild."

"No way. There are cougars hiding in the bushes."

Leta starts to laugh but instead she smiles. "You just moved here, didn't you?"

"Nearly three months ago."

"Where'd you live before?"

"The city."

"How come you moved here?"

"For my dad to have horses, like when he was growing up. And because we boys just get into trouble in the city. That's why nobody ever comes to our farm, so we stay out of trouble."

Leta laughs. "You'd never get into trouble."

One day when I get off the bus Leta is not there.

Henry laughs. "Such a long face, Oliver. She's just out riding Prince. Giving him his exercise. She'll have to bring a friend sometime so she can walk both horses at the same time."

Mom opens the door. "Is he bothering you, Henry?"

"Not at all, Ellie," Henry says. He reaches up and grabs hold of a good apple. He looks right at the apple and says quietly, "Loosen up, Your Highness," and then twists it off. He likes to give the apples names. Sometimes he calls them Big Sweetie or Juicy Girl. He rubs the apple on his shirt, gives me a big smile, and hands it down to me.

I put the apple in the front pocket of my hoodie and then

fill the bruised apple bucket till Mom calls me in for dinner. Benny meets me in the bathroom. He stands to the side to let me go first and then says, "After you, Blue." I kick him hard on his shin and hurt my toe. He grins wickedly and says, "Try again. Come on."

I want it to hurt him one day, not me.

We sit down at the table with Mom, and Benny says, "Dad at another meeting?" Then he uses his fork like a front-end loader and shovels mashed potatoes into his mouth.

"Slow down, Benny," Mom says.

Benny says something with his mouth stuffed with potatoes, and Mom says, "Again? You went to Matthew's yesterday."

"Mom, I'm so far from my friends out here. It's not my fault we hadta move."

"Whose fault is it?" I ask.

"You don't know anything, do you," Benny says.

"Benny!" Mom says. She's mad. Her cheeks are hard and red, like a shiny apple.

"Whatever," Benny says. "Can you drive me to Matthew's?"

"It's only two fields over," she says. "You can walk over and I'll get you later."

When he goes, Mom says, "C'mere, Oliver," and I sit on her lap. She likes to cuddle me all the time.

"How come we moved here?" I ask her.

"I told you. It's a great place for a boy to grow up," Mom says.

"Now it's just us and a bunch of dumb coyotes, Ellie," I say in Dad's voice, and she laughs the way she used to, when Dad said so many funny things. He forgot all his funny things a long time ago.

One day Leta's friend Amy comes, and Dad comes home early and shows them how to hitch Anthony to the cart. He tells them to be very careful. "A horse is fine in his own environment," he says, "but you never can tell how a horse might react out there on the roads."

Leta steers Anthony down our lane and onto the gravel road. We stop at the first road and wait for a pickup truck to pass. In the beginning I count the roads we go down, but after four or five I lose track. It seems like ages because of all the waiting for the trucks that stir up the dust, but finally we get to the Shell station on the highway.

Leta holds the reins while Amy takes me inside to pick out some candy. There's gum. Chocolate bars. Fizzing candy. Suckers. Jawbreakers. Life Savers. I slide my finger over the shiny wrappers until Amy says, "Come *on*, Oliver!"

I pick the tiny candies that explode when you put them in your mouth. Amy buys some Sweethearts candies and we go back to the cart.

"You're too sweet, Oliver," Leta says. "Have another Sweetheart." She hands me a yellow one. "I wish all boys were as sweet as you."

"I'm the sweetest boy in our family," I say. I hold the Sweetheart down with my tongue. When I take the candy out of my mouth, the word looks funny. "My mom says so," I say.

"Your mom says so?" Leta says. "Then it must be true."

"Yep. She's never going to let me go away."

"Never?" Leta says.

I shake my head no.

"Hey, let's pretend you're our little boy," Amy says. "And you're so cute, we'll let you do whatever you want."

"I want to steer," I say.

Leta laughs and says, "No way."

"Oh, come on, just let him. We're right here," Amy says. Then she makes Leta's name into a song: *Leee-taaa.*

Leta has a think and then she puts the reins in my hands. She holds on for a bit before letting go.

"Yay, yay!" I yell. I steer for a long time. Leta helps me at the turns.

"I'll bet your dad looked just like you when he was little," Leta says. "He's cute, your dad."

"Wouldn't you like to ride with him?" Amy asks. "In the cart?"

Leta doesn't say anything.

"You're dying for a little kiss, I know you are. Just one little kiss."

I shake the reins to make Anthony go faster. They won't notice because they are giggling. Leta is laughing so hard she's bent over.

"Let's give him something special," Leta says.

"Maybe a cigar," says Amy.

"We'd have to hide it."

"Smoking is bad," I say, and they stop giggling and look at me. I put on my Mom voice and frown hard, like I'm Mom talking to Dad, and I make my voice sound really high and say, "You keep smoking, Philip, and you'll have a heart attack before you're fifty."

Leta asks, "Hey, what does your dad like, Oliver?"

"Peanuts. The salty kind."

"That's boring," Leta says. "What else?"

"Horses. Horses are his best friend," I say. Then I shout: "Beer!"

"Hey, Oliver," Leta says all of a sudden. She stops giggling and looks serious. "This is girl talk. It's just talk, not real. It's our secret, right?" She keeps saying "Right, Oliver?" and poking my belly until I say "Right."

"But," Leta whispers, "it's got to be something Ellie wouldn't give him. Something she wouldn't think of."

Anthony trots off the road and bumps into the ditch. "Yahoo!" I yell. I laugh and shake the reins hard. Leta takes them and gives a quick yank that makes Anthony stop so fast I nearly bounce off. Amy grabs my arm. Then she hops down with Leta.

"Hold the side," Leta says to me. "Hold on tight."

Amy pushes the cart and Leta pulls Anthony. They push and pull and finally get Anthony and the cart and me out of the ditch and onto the gravel road. Leta's face is red and frowning, like Mom's when she's mad. Leta and Amy don't say anything all the way home. They don't even look at each other or have any more candies.

We unhitch Anthony and put the cart in the end stall. We're brushing him when Dad gets home. Leta goes over to him and tells him about going into the ditch.

"Was anyone hurt?" he asks. When Leta says no, he says, "What about Anthony? Is the cart damaged?"

"No," Leta says.

"Well, it's all right then, isn't it? Oliver," Dad says. "Go over and pick some apples." I go and pick the bruised ones off the ground. I can't hear him, but I know he's telling them it's okay because now they're all laughing. When I turn to look at them, I don't think it's Dad. There's something different about him. They're all talking quietly and smiling. After a minute he comes over to me and takes me inside.

"Ellie," he says, and he starts to laugh like he's just seen the funniest thing ever. "You won't believe what those girls got up to."

"Well, what?" Mom says.

"They"—he bends over and holds his side—"they ended up in the ditch with Anthony. You should have seen their faces, Ellie!"

"In the ditch?" Mom says. "Wasn't Oliver with them?"

"Yep," I say. I watch for her to laugh. Any second she'll be laughing too.

"Oliver! What happened?"

"I was steering and we were playing I was their little boy—"

"They gave you the reins?" Mom screams. "Philip! You did talk to them, didn't you? I don't see what's so funny about this."

Dad makes his lips go into a straight line and tries hard not to laugh but I can see he's got some of the funny left in his cheeks because they're wobbly. "Talk to them?" he says. "Of course I did."

"Stupid girls. Stupid, careless, irresponsible girls. I hope you told them not to take the pony and cart out anymore."

"Aw, Ellie. They're just kids. There was no harm done."

"Philip," Mom says. She walks outside loudly and the door slams after her.

"Wait here, Oliver," Dad says. "I shouldn't have told her.

I thought she'd find it funny." He runs his fingers through his hair.

I watch from the window beside the door. She talks to them for a long time and when she's done, she comes in without waiting for them to say anything, and then Dad goes out.

I know he'll tell them not to worry, not to listen to her, she'll come around, they're not stupid and careless and irresponsible, like Mom said. Leta was looking down at the ground for a long time, but now she's smiling at him. Dad is smiling too. He's got on a big happy face. Dad always fixes everything. In a little while he'll fix things with Mom too.

Then Dad comes inside. Mom doesn't say anything and he doesn't say anything either, but they both look at each other like they have lots to say but they have to go away and have a think first.

I go outside and walk around behind the stable. Leta and Amy are sitting on the mound with their sticks and making stick people and silly faces. I know something is different, but I don't know what. I sit right on Leta's lap, and she gives me a hug and smiles. I don't want Henry to come and take her home yet. I don't want to go back inside and have Mom hold me so hard I can't breathe.

Leta has been with us a month. I know because Mom says it at breakfast. "She arrived September 30," Mom says. "One month today."

I look at Dad to see what he'll say. He'll probably say something like, "A month already?" Or, "Imagine that!" But he keeps on eating his cereal.

"Dad," I say, "did you look like me when you were little?"

Dad looks at me closely. "A bit," he says.

"Am I sweet?"

Dad laughs. "Most definitely. Why?"

"Leta thinks I'm as sweet as you," I say, and wait for him to laugh again, but all he does is look slowly over at Mom and then look away quickly. He doesn't say anything. He just puts down his cereal bowl.

After a minute Dad says, "I have to go now." He gets up and goes over to kiss Mom like he does every morning, but she turns her head away so he blows her a kiss and waves goodbye and goes out to his car.

"Those girls are a little silly about Dad," Benny says.

"What does that mean?" Mom asks.

"I dunno," Benny says. He picks up his cereal bowl and drinks the rest of his milk.

"Yeah," I say. I want to tell about the present for Dad but I remember Leta made me promise not to say anything.

"Hurry, boys," Mom says. "Time to catch your bus."

After school I find Leta and Amy in the back of Chuck's stall. I stand in the doorway and watch them take off his saddle and bridle and brush his sweat. I'm very quiet so they won't see me. I like to listen to them talk about Dad. When they say his name, they make it sound like a word on a Sweethearts candy. Then they smile and their lips are like waves—one smile starts and then a bigger one comes and then one even bigger. They talk about his hair, how they like his hair. He has little curly bits over his forehead and something they call his five o'clock shadow; they love that.

When Mom talks about Dad's hair, she says it needs a trim. Or he needs to shave. He shouldn't be seen with that awful stubble, she says.

"I like Philip soooo much," Leta says. Her eyes flutter. Amy whispers things in Leta's ear. Leta's face turns pink and her eyes open wide, and she squeals and tells Amy she's got butterflies all over. Amy laughs.

I know about nervous butterflies. I get them in my stomach sometimes when I have to talk to scary people. These are different though. These are happy butterflies that tickle your belly and make you want to run around and dance. When I see Leta and Amy up close like this, I remember what Dad's face looked like when he was talking to them after the cart went into the ditch and he told me to go pick apples—he had the happy butterflies. His eyes were shining, and they were fluttery like Leta's and Amy's are now.

I hear a slow *crunch-crunch* on the gravel, and there's Mom standing right beside me. Leta and Amy don't see. Mom doesn't say hello to them. She doesn't call me to come in for a snack or say it's homework time. She just stands beside me and looks in with her eyes so squinty I don't think she can see through them. It's just straw back there, I want to tell her, but I'm being very quiet so Leta and Amy don't know I'm there.

"You're baa-ad," Amy says, and shrieks. "Remember when he came out to talk to us and he—" Then she sees Mom and her mouth makes an O and her eyes get very big.

"I know, when he touched my arm. If only I'd—"

Amy kicks Leta with her big boot, hard. It's a good kick and it hurts. Leta makes a face and yells, "Ouch! What was that for?" Then she sees Mom, too. For a long time all you can hear are Chuck's stomping and snorting. Leta and Amy stare down at the muck and straw around their boots.

Mom's face is like a mask that's stuck on. It's like she's gone, even though her eyes are moving back and forth from Leta to Amy. And then she looks at me and says, "Come inside, Oliver." Her voice is so mad I'm sure I'm in trouble. But when I get out of the stall, she steps in and says in a quiet, angry voice, "You ladies can both go home now. You don't need to come back."

Mom pulls me by the arm to the house. I'm so mad at her for telling them they can't come back I could spit.

Inside, Mom tells me to do my reading. She doesn't sit next to me or put a peanut butter sandwich at my place. She doesn't even start dinner. Instead, she walks to the living room and comes back to the kitchen. She opens the fridge and closes it. She goes to the window and looks out. Then she comes back to the table and looks over my shoulder.

"He'd better come home soon," Mom says and slams a cupboard door.

"Who?" I ask.

"Your father, that's who."

"Oh, Dad. Well, he'll fix everything, won't he?" I say. "I know he'll fix things so Leta and Amy come back, too."

"Yes, he will fix things," Mom says angrily.

When Benny and Dad come home, Mom gives us leftover

noodles. She sits with us, but she doesn't eat anything. When I go to bed I hear her talking to Dad. She's talking and he's listening. Her voice starts out soft, like always, and slowly gets louder. After a long time of listening, it's Dad's turn. He says only one thing: "Nothing is happening, except in your imagination."

Then I hear the front door open and close and feet crunching on the gravel near the stable.

My door opens, and Mom comes over to my bed and kisses me on the cheek. I'm still mad about Mom making Leta and Amy leave.

"Mom," I say. "Do you get the happy butterflies with Dad?"

Mom laughs quietly through her sad face. "The what?"

"What Dad and Amy and Leta get. Smoochy all over, from your head to your toes," I say, "and a tickling feeling inside. Like that night we went into the ditch and he fixed things with them. Dad got the happy butterflies." Mom is looking at me now but she isn't saying anything, so I say, "When you get the happy butterflies, you give the other person special things. Amy and Leta have something special to give Dad. They can't leave till they give it to him."

"What do they want to give Dad?"

"I don't know. Not peanuts or beer, they said. Not the boring stuff you give him. They said it was something you don't have," I say. I look at her for a minute and then say, "They're so pretty, aren't they?" Then I remember promising not to say anything, so I turn onto my side with my back to her and close my eyes.

🐦 NO MATTER HOW NICEY-
NICEY THE PARENTS WERE

She'd found the hat back in January in the little gift shop below her apartment. It wasn't the cold that drew her to it; it was the feel of the fabric. The hat was thin and red and silky and didn't make her head itch. Leanne couldn't take any sort of itch, especially on her head. Ever since she found the hat, she'd worn it all the time, except when she was in the shower.

When she went for the interview, the people wouldn't stop looking at her hat. They kept stealing little looks at her head. They didn't say anything, but clearly they were bothered. Maybe they thought she should take it off. It was summer, and *he* was in shorts and a tucked-in checkered T-shirt, and *she* was wearing a short, sleeveless sundress. They should know that everyone feels things differently.

The baby was in his crib. Leanne wanted to pick him up and hold him and run her fingers over the fine, dark down on his head. She hated this part, the beginning. She wanted it to be over and done with so she could be alone with him.

"He's sleeping," the mother said when Leanne asked to hold him, though she could see that.

The mother was named for a month, June. When she heard the name, Leanne thought of the start of summer and sunshine, of new buds and a lightness in the air. The mother didn't seem summerish to Leanne. June was about thirty years old. She was the business type, smart looking and neat. Her sundress was turquoise with yellow and green swirls. She had thick, short hair and small pearly earrings. So stylish. Leanne guessed she was probably the sort who wore things for a year and then passed them on. "We don't pick him up when he's sleeping."

The father smiled in a friendly way. After a few minutes Leanne noticed that he smiled all the time, and it made her wonder whether he really was friendly or if he just came with that sort of face. It was a pleasant smile, though, and it made her feel welcome. His name was Christian. Whenever Leanne heard that name, she wondered if the person *was* a Christian. He might be, but if he was not, having a name like that made him someone to be wary of. He bobbed his head up and down and said maybe after, if the baby woke, Leanne could hold him. Leanne found herself nodding in the same way to keep up with him, and then she looked down at the baby. His skin was slightly pink and he wore nothing but a cloth diaper. She hated cloth. It meant safety pins. Safety pins could go right through skin just like that, and before you knew it a tiny ball of blood would burst out, round and warm and wet.

They'd said on the phone the baby was six months old. June was going back to work fulltime. They didn't want to take him to someone else's home; they wanted someone to come in. You could tell they had money because of how the room was done up. Leanne took it all in so she could describe it to Simon later when she got home. The crib had padding all around it, and the fabric on the padding had teddy bears in blue sailor suits. There was a mobile over the crib, the kind you could wind up to make music, with bears facing down at the baby. They were sailor bears, the same as on the crib padding and the quilt and the curtains and the wall trim. That's how you could tell. Everything matched. There was a rocking chair near the crib where the mother and father probably took turns sitting with the baby.

The next thing Leanne knew the mother was walking down the hall. The father turned to Leanne and gestured toward the open door. All three of them walked single file down the hall till they were back by the front door. Leanne looked into the living room, at the soft, white couch and huge leather chairs and the tall purple-and-green glass vase on the coffee table. She knew what was coming next: the parents would sit on the big chairs and she would sit on the couch and they would ask questions. The room was begging her to come in and sprawl on the couch and close her eyes. That would come later. For now, once they were all sitting down, she would look around without making it obvious. Everything here was tidy and nice, even nicer than in the shop where she found the hat.

But nobody sat. The mother turned to Leanne and said, "You said on the phone you're at university."

"I'm getting my Education degree. Same as Simon. We'll both be finished at the same time."

"Who's Simon?" the mother asked.

"He's my..." Leanne thought quickly. She'd moved in with Simon after they had left Moose Jaw. Some people were particular about that sort of thing. She knew the word "husband" wouldn't sound right coming from her lips, so she said, "We're married," and casually slipped her left hand behind her back so they wouldn't see that she didn't have a ring. She could say she'd left it in the bathroom, if they asked. She and Simon were as good as married. "As soon as we both have good jobs," Simon had said, "then we'll tie the knot."

"Since you're at university, are you available during the day, then?" the father asked.

"I take my classes at night," Leanne said. "Simon, too, because he's working. He doesn't want to take out any loans. They get you when you pay them back. By the time you pay them back you've paid for your degree twice over."

"Education," Christian said.

Leanne nodded. She hoped they didn't ask where. She was really at the college because she couldn't get into university, and it was just a certificate program, but it was all about the same in the end.

"What year are you in?" Christian asked.

"First. We just started."

The mother looked at her. She had a way of looking that made Leanne feel she was trying to see inside her. Her eyes were clear and brown. When she stared at Leanne, her eyes didn't move; they didn't even blink. No, there was nothing summerish about her. She was too cold. After a few seconds the mother looked quickly up at Leanne's hat and her eyes darted over Leanne's face and she asked, "Do you have your references?"

"The thing is, we moved here from Moose Jaw and that's where all my references are. I don't have the phone numbers anymore. But I looked after babies and toddlers and older children too, all the time." The parents looked at each other and didn't say anything, so she told them she was the oldest in her family and that she looked after her little brother and sister too, way back. But her mother was dead now and in the grave in Moose Jaw, so she couldn't give her mother's name as a reference.

For the first time, the father stopped smiling.

"Gosh, sorry about your mother," he said. He sounded so truly sorry Leanne was nearly struck dumb. He hadn't known her mother. Most people were like that, people she hardly knew. The one thing she'd learned to say back was "Me too," and she said it now, even though she didn't know exactly what she felt.

"Well," the father said. "Maybe you could tell us what you'd do if Andrew cried. That's one thing we wanted to ask." He glanced at the mother, and then back at Leanne. *As if he's unsure,* Leanne thought. But then the mother nodded, and Leanne knew she was saying, without saying it: Yes, that's what we wanted to ask.

It was pretty clear to Leanne what was happening: June and Christian were new parents who were smart about their work but had no idea what they were doing when it came to babies and needed someone to come in and help them. "You just find out if he's hungry or has a dirty diaper, that's all. A diaper will make him uncomfortable, but he doesn't have the words to say it. But I would get rid of those cloth diapers. They just give the baby a rash." It was really the disposables that did, but Leanne didn't want to be near pins. She couldn't see pins without seeing the little drop of blood on that tiny baby. That baby had grown into a little girl and then a bigger girl and had even hugged Leanne, but Leanne couldn't look at her without seeing that bawling red face and, worse, remembering herself standing at the change table, flooded with such a curious feeling at what she'd done and being so afraid she'd do it again, right then, just because.

"Cloth diapers?" the mother said. She looked surprised, so Leanne knew that this was news to her. She also knew there were the types who had to hold their babies all the time and the types who left babies to sort themselves out on their own and just cry. These were the two camps, when it came to babies, and she tried to find out as soon as she could where the parents stood.

"Yes," Leanne said, and then, "Usually you leave babies to cry," she added, guessing they were in that camp. "If it's not a dirty diaper, that is."

"You do?" the mother said. "What would you do if Andrew didn't *stop* crying?"

"Come on now," the father said, and Leanne thought he was reproaching June on her behalf. She liked him for that. "That's not really a fair question. That's not about to happen."

"It might," the mother snapped and looked hard at him.

The father smiled and tipped his head to one side as if to say he didn't agree. The other thing Leanne knew, after all those years babysitting all those kids in Moose Jaw, was that no matter what, no matter how nicey-nicey the parents were at the start, there was always something else going on that they tried to cover up. They always disagreed about something and weren't as lovey-dovey as they first seemed. Sometimes it came out right off; other times, not for seven or eight months. The longer it took, the more the parents didn't really like each other.

"Do you have first aid training?" the mother asked.

Leanne nodded.

"Do you like walking?"

"Walking?"

"Would you take Andrew out in the stroller? He likes that."

"Oh, I love walking. I'm always out walking. It's my favourite thing." Leanne hated walking, but she had learned that you could say pretty much anything in an interview and it didn't really matter.

The mother looked at Leanne's fingernails. "I have to ask if you smoke. We can't have a smoker."

"Even if I did, I would never smoke around a baby. Those tiny little lungs can't take it."

The mother and the father looked at each other and both nodded as if to say they knew what she meant.

"Do you drive?" the father asked.

"Sure, but it's not like we'll be going anywhere," Leanne said. She would just hang out here, as far as she could tell. With the soft baby.

"In case there's an emergency," the father said. "And one of us can't get home in time."

"Oh," said Leanne.

"Do you have a car?" the mother asked.

"No. Oh, I mean yes. It's Simon's, but we share it."

"So you wouldn't have it here, then?" the mother asked. She looked very worried now, and it made Leanne wonder how often there was an emergency.

"I can arrange it," Leanne said, though Simon would never agree to it. He didn't agree to anything anymore.

"Well, then. What do you like most about babies?" the mother said. She smiled. It was almost a teasing smile, like Leanne was being set up. Like the mother was really asking something else.

Leanne knew they'd saved this question for last. It was the hardest one to answer because they were the parents and it was their first baby, so they would have one right answer and there were probably a hundred wrong ones. She looked at the mother for a long time, wondering what the mother was looking for. The mother stared back calmly. Her eyes and face were completely blank.

Finally, Leanne said, proudly, because she knew she couldn't go wrong, "Everything. I like everything about babies."

"Come on, everything?" the father asked. He laughed. "Even the diaper changing?"

"Sure. That's part and parcel of having a baby." She could tell they didn't like that part, and then she knew there were other things about having a baby they didn't like. Maybe that's why they were both going to be at work and not at home with the baby. But the way the father had laughed made her laugh, too. She was totally relaxed around them now, almost like she'd known them forever, and she wanted them to know how much she liked babies so she said, "Simon and I are going to have a baby. Not yet, but soon. Simon wants to wait till we're both done and working, but I don't want to wait that long and besides, I'm the one who takes the pill every month so I'll just"—she held up both hands and curled the first two fingers of each hand to make quotation marks—"forget"—she lowered her hands—"a few times and then tell him the pill is not a hundred per cent like it says on the package, and he'll never know. Accidents happen all the time, right?"

The mother opened her mouth a little in surprise and then gave a quick nod, and her eyes gave a little flick, an aha, like she got it. As far as Leanne could tell, it only meant one thing—it meant they'd finally connected, that they were on the same page. Maybe the mother had "forgotten" herself, or had at least thought about it and wished she had. Maybe she had never pulled one over on Christian like that, but deep down she wanted to; Leanne could see that. She could see by the way June rolled her lips in till you almost couldn't see the red and glanced over at Christian. Leanne tried not to look at him because she didn't want to embarrass them or let on that she'd found them out. But she felt more sure of herself now. She had an in. They'd have a spat about taking her, after she left, but the mother would find a way to persuade him. She could tell.

Leanne took a deep breath and glanced leisurely into the living room. For the first time she noticed the shawl, draped over the back of the couch. It was knitted or maybe crocheted, with big loops, dark green and soft and gorgeous. She'd look stunning in it. Simon would really warm to her in that. He wouldn't be so freaked out anymore. Maybe things would go so well the mother would let her have it, after a time. The mother had so many nice things. She would think so well of Leanne that she would just pass things on to her.

"So, you know," the father said, "Andrew's always yanking at things," he said. "June can't wear earrings around him. Heck, I've stopped wearing mine altogether." He gave a loud laugh, and Leanne didn't know if he really wore earrings or was pulling her leg. "Would it bother you if he pulled your hat off?" He grinned. The grin made her feel a bit uncomfortable; she couldn't tell if it was a friendly grin or not. He really wanted to know about the hat, or have her take it off. That was it. Leanne knew it was because of what had happened between her and the mother. Because she'd figured them out. And now, he had to get in his dig. Maybe he wasn't the kind man she thought he was.

Leanne put her hand to her head. It would be sweet, if the baby pulled her hat off. He'd pat her fuzzy head and laugh and drool and pat his own velvety head and then pat hers again. She'd let him do it whenever he wanted. Maybe he'd do it all the time, because she would hold him all the time and let him nuzzle into her and fall asleep on her. She would let him do that. She would be closer to him than his real mother was. That was the best part, being the one the baby wanted to be with most. It was easy. Babies didn't care how you looked. They didn't care about hair the way adults did. Andrew wouldn't care that her hair used to be like his mother's, only longer, halfway down her back once. Simon used to love running his fingers through her hair and taking her head in his hands to kiss her. Then she got sick, and her hair got so thin and patchy and ugly looking she'd finally taken the scissors to it. She loved her new look, the short spiky hair sticking out here and there, till Simon appeared and said, "You look like a freak."

She looked at her hacked-up hair and remembered it was Christmas Eve and they were going to someone's house and she was supposed to make something, some side dish with a strange name, with an au gratin or du monde that she had no clue how to make. The only thing that could save her look was the razor. *Zmm, zmm, zmm.* She had thought her hair would grow back, but it never really did. Sometimes that happened, her doctor had said. She found the hat maybe two days later. It was so perfect, she knew she couldn't leave the store without slipping it into her sleeve. She felt sick to her stomach whenever she remembered taking it and swore over and over she would never do such a thing again. But it held her head so perfectly, like a pair of huge, warm hands.

The baby let out a howl, and they all looked down the hall, surprised. Both the mother and the father started down the hall, then looked at each other before turning to Leanne.

Leanne watched the mother, waiting for her to say she could stay. Now, today. Because they really needed her. But the mother said tersely, "Thank you for coming," and hurried to the baby's room. The father looked after her and then opened the door for Leanne.

Leanne glanced over at the shawl and the stunning red jacket in the closet. The baby continued to holler.

"I have to go," the father said. "Please." He gestured toward the open doorway.

They really needed her. It wouldn't be long now. Leanne said goodbye to the father and stepped outside. It would only be a matter of time before the mother called.

❧ BANANA AND SPLIT

Kate was cycling to work when her sister called. Kate hadn't thought of Liz for more than three weeks. It could go like this sometimes; she could convince herself, some days, that Liz—and, of course, Haley—did not exist. Kate had made them up and then—snap!—made them disappear. But all it took was a certain turn of a head, hair pushed off a cheek just so, a whiff of flowery perfume, and in an instant Liz was right there and Haley was curled up between them. And then came that awful ache around her heart, her chest, even her jawbone. You're a grinder, her dentist told her once. After a time, when the ache lessened, Kate would go over in her mind what she'd say if she ran into Liz in the street or in the library. But Liz lived in Fort McMurray now. She'd moved there nine years ago, just months after the last time they were all together at Mom and Dad's. Kate had never been invited up to Fort Mac. And Liz wouldn't go to Mom and Dad's when Kate went up on weekends. So she'd fantasize about talking to her on the phone. Mom had given Kate the number ages ago. She would say right off the bat, before the hello even, that she hadn't done anything. And Liz would say: "I know."

But Kate never called. Instead, she succumbed to the huge cloud of anger about the stupid stupid stupidness of it all. And inevitably, the sadness hit her, the wearying sadness she carried everywhere. It had burrowed deep inside, in its own little sack, but on some days she thought the sadness was outside her body and everyone could see it. She imagined it as a small grey helium balloon tied to the top loop of her backpack. No matter how fast she pedalled or where she went, the balloon followed her, a warm, sagging mass.

Kate could not help feeling smug as she sailed past the slow-moving morning traffic on her Trek hybrid. Then she heard the wasp behind her neck, and her smugness was replaced with annoyance. The wasp had worked its way into the side pocket of her backpack. It would be screaming mad if it didn't get out soon. Kate pedalled hard to the next red light and slipped off her pack.

It wasn't a wasp. It was the darn cell phone. She hated the cell phone. She had bought it only after Mom had insisted she get it for her road trips. You and your bike rides, Mom had said. What if something happens and you're all on your own a long way from anywhere? A pretty young woman, alone on the roads. You have to take some precautions, Katie.

She pulled the phone from the side pocket of her pack and flipped it open. The display read *Cox, Liz.* Kate's heart sped up. The phone had stopped buzzing. She pushed a few buttons to retrieve the message and slipped the phone under her helmet and listened. There was nothing, not even Liz's breathing.

The light changed. She put the phone back and cycled on.

Liz wouldn't call. She'd never call. Probably it was another Liz Cox. But it was Mom's sixty-fifth coming up. Maybe Liz was planning a party, like she had for Mom's fiftieth. Maybe she'd come. With Haley.

There it was again, that squeezing around her heart.

Haley would be graduating from high school this year. It was already halfway through June; maybe the graduation ceremony had already happened. No. Kate's parents would have mentioned it. They told her everything about Haley. When Haley joined Scouts. When she got her first road bike. Mom showed Kate all the school photos—a girl with long brown hair, uneven bangs, and a big grin wearing blue jean overalls and a striped shirt. A regular kid. She could be anybody's kid. But she wasn't. And all of a sudden, for the school picture, Haley was wearing eyeliner and lip gloss. Kate almost couldn't look. She had been there when Haley was born, right there in the hospital room, less than three feet away from all that gooey blood. She'd said yes as soon as Liz asked. Gary couldn't be there. Kate knew why; they all knew why, though nobody talked about it. He was off with his buddies, at the bar. So Kate was the first to hold Haley, the first to change her puny diaper.

She rode over to Liz's every day the first two weeks, just to be with Haley. It wasn't that Gary was out with the guys and Liz needed an extra set of hands; Mom was there, too. It wasn't that Kate was a baby person; she was not. It was just that there was something about the little elf of a child she couldn't get enough of.

Kate locked her bike outside the Extension Building. By nine o'clock she was at her desk, facing her computer screen and watching it flash through its slow start-up. She'd been teaching E S L and co-ordinating the program for close to seven years. She was proud of this, even when Dad made his wise-cracks about her job.

"You still in that job at the uneeversitee, Katie?" he'd asked two weekends ago when she was up for a visit.

"Oh Dad." She rolled her eyes. She hated the way he said "university." "What, you think I should quit and move back in here?"

"You'll never find a man with a job like that, you know."

"Bill," Mom said. She gave him a look that said *enough*.

"Just sayin.' You shouldn't be too smart if you're a woman."

"She'll be just as smart as she likes, with or without a man." Mom's cheeks went suddenly pink.

"Let's change the subject," Kate said. She knew it bothered them, that she hadn't brought home a boyfriend. That she didn't even talk about boys. She was twenty-nine. She wondered when parents stopped thinking about whether their kids would go out with someone. "Settle down," as Mom put it. Mom and Dad would probably have liked Colin, the guy in her anthropology class who had asked her out once. She'd almost said yes, when he had asked. He looked nice enough. But instead she'd just shaken her head, no. How would she know? How would she ever know what he was really like? After she said no the first time, it was easy. It wasn't long before guys stopped asking.

The office phone rang. She glanced at the phone's display and picked up the receiver.

"Hi, Mom," she said. She tucked the phone onto her

shoulder, double-clicked her email icon, and typed the password. Mom would remind Kate that she hadn't been up for a visit in close to two months. Ask why she couldn't come up instead of going biking all weekend.

"Kate, listen, Liz's trying to reach you. You have to talk to her."

The phone fell onto Kate's lap. She could almost see the hand moving toward her heart to give it a squeeze. She retrieved the phone.

"Are you there? Haley's gone missing."

"What?"

"Haley's gone missing."

"Oh my God." Kate felt dizzy. She heard Dad's words: *There go Mac and Tosh.* And: *Well, if it isn't Banana and Split.* She didn't want to think about what Haley was like as an eighteen-year-old. Maybe a punster, like Liz. Or secretive. Like Gary.

"She had two weeks to go in high school. She went out what, three nights ago, and that was it, boom, just like that. No sign of her. They've called everyone. It's with the RCMP now. I tried to call you all weekend but you weren't answering your phone."

"I was on a road trip," Kate said quietly. She'd seen that her mother had called, four times at least, but she'd gotten in so late last night she didn't want to call. She looked up and saw her boss, Ellen, standing near her open doorway.

"I wish I knew what happened between you two. You used to be so close, you adored her, she doted on you, even though she was so stinkin' mad when you came along. She was eight when you were born, remember?"

"Geez Mom, I know. Why are you telling me this?" Kate had heard her mother tell the story so many times, how everyone used to laugh at the way she trotted around after Liz. Like Liz was her mother.

"Listen, you, Dad told me this morning that if you two don't kiss and make up pretty damn quick, he won't have either of you back in this house, he's so fed up with the two of you. I put my foot down and told him that's not how it is in my house. You girls need a home, you always have a home here. You have to put your foot down with a man, Kate. That's Liz's problem right there, she never put her foot down."

"Mom, I'm at work—"

"Call Liz. She'll tell you. I'm hanging up now."

Ellen knocked lightly on Kate's door before walking in. She was squat and greying. Kate watched her speak but had no real sense of what she was saying. Information about program changes, class schedules, a meeting. A student was waiting in the hall. Could Kate deal with his concerns right away. Kate nodded and waited for Ellen to leave.

The student came in. A young man from China in his first year of the doctoral program. His English was not good. At one time Kate thought she should learn Mandarin. She'd enrolled in a class and attended religiously for weeks. What a hopeless case. She gave up after failing the first test and decided to be very patient and listen well. If only she could understand what the student was saying. Luckily, he was kind. He said he would come back later.

Ellen walked briskly back into Kate's office, her skirt whooshing, and said something that sounded like she wanted Kate to shred the hoya plant in the corner.

"What did you say?" Kate said.

Ellen looked closely at her. "Are you all right?"

Kate nodded. Ellen gave her a curious look and left. Kate's hands were puffy and warm. The nerves in her stomach were leaping up to her throat.

The last time Kate had seen Haley, the girl should have pranced around like a gazelle and jumped up onto Kate's lap and played the one thousand kisses game. But that hadn't happened, that last weekend at Mom and Dad's. Kate was still a student then. She had stayed up too late during the week and crashed when she came home. She slept in, that last day they were all together.

Kate knew that while she slept, Liz would probably be cooking sausages, Haley would be making toast, and Mom would be cracking eggs for omelettes. Dad would likely park himself at the table to drink coffee and read the paper. Gary would be sprawled on the couch with his BlackBerry. When Kate came down from her old bedroom at the far end of the upstairs hall, she would set the table, and Haley would skip over to her and dance around her and entangle her long arms and legs into Kate's and giggle when Dad said, "Which one of you's Mac and which one's Tosh, I want to know." Later, Haley would find the chocolate eggs Kate and Liz had hidden the night before, then line them up by colour and size, count them, share them. They would snuggle up on the couch to watch *Matilda*, Haley's favourite movie.

When Kate finally made her way to the table, she saw that it had already been set. She looked at the eggs and toast on her plate and wanted to throw up. Mom told them all to eat, eat up. Kate swallowed hard and fought the urge to be sick. Only Dad and Gary were hungry. Starving, by the way they ate. No one said anything, except Mom, who asked why they were all so quiet on such a beautiful Easter morning. When Kate looked across the table at Haley, she saw the girl staring back at her as if she already knew what Kate didn't know—that this would be the last time they would see each other. As soon as Gary had wolfed down his last bite of sausage, Liz stood, told Gary and Haley to get up and say goodbye, and whooshed them out the front door.

Kate rooted through her backpack for the slip of paper with her sister's number that Mom had shoved at her years ago. She picked up the phone, set it against her ear, listened to the dial tone for several seconds, and then hung up.

She felt as if she had a tape wedged somewhere in the back of her head and once a day hit the "play" button, torturing herself with that last morning when they were all at home. She was sleeping lightly, drifting in and out of dreams, and aware of the sounds from downstairs. Ordinary sounds, the clink of forks on plates, of spoons against coffee cups—sounds that made their way into her sleep and that she remembered when she woke. The hard scrape of chairs on linoleum. Mom's quick footsteps moving between the fridge and the

stove. Dad's slippered feet shuffling to the table. A chair being pulled out. Soft morning voices. These were cosy home
sounds, sounds that drifted up to her, permeated her skin,
became part of her physical memory of home. Clink, scrape,
slip slide, laugh.

Kate picked up the phone again and dialled slowly. Before
the first ring finished, the phone was picked up.

"Hello."

"Liz?"

"Kate." Liz was curt. As if she were talking to a stranger.

Kate thought if she hadn't been asleep, if she had been
awake and seen him coming, if only if only if only, she would
have said something or done something. Of course she would
have. But she had been asleep. She thought she was dreaming,
at first, when she felt his fingers squeezing her head. Then his
lips pushed against hers until her teeth cut through the inside
of her lower lip and she felt the strange, almost pleasant wet
warmth of blood. His body smelled of the cologne that made
her gag and his cheeks scratched. He didn't shave on Sundays.

"Is she there?" Liz demanded.

If she had been fully awake, his hands would not have
found their way under the quilt to her bare breasts. But there
she was, sleeping on her back, naked. His fingers, strong as
iron on her head, became feathers when they found her
breasts, light, fluttering wisps. Even his body quaked all over.
She opened her eyes and grabbed his hands. Then he came
down hard, so hard she sat up to push him away. In the pushing, her face was in his neck. Her hands and arms were tan-
gled into his.

"What?" Kate asked.

"Haley. Is she with you?" Liz said.

"Haley?" Kate said. "No. Why are you asking me?"

"She wanted to come to you," Liz said. "She'd been asking for I don't know how many months. She wouldn't stop
asking."

"She's not here." Kate's heart had given a little leap of de-
light at the thought of Haley wanting to come see her. But

she couldn't shake the feeling of unease that crawled over her skin as well.

Liz's cheerful shout came first from the bottom of the stairs—*Kaaay-teee!*—then from the hallway—*Kaaay-teee!*—and finally, right outside the door: "*Kaaay-teee!!*"

When Liz walked in, Gary pushed Kate down on the bed and growled through clenched teeth, "For God's sake, I said stop!" He stood up straight, patted his shirt, and smoothed his hair.

"Katie, didn't you hear?" Liz said. "I've been calling you—uh, what's going on here?"

Kate pulled the quilt up over her chest. She heard the chirping through the window that she'd left open a crack the night before. Robins already, calling to each other. They seemed so loud and happy. Kate didn't hear birds in the city; there were always apartment noises, like water in the pipes or a noisy furnace or shouts from the two people who lived next door. She tried hard to turn away from Liz, but Liz's stare took her in, every bit of her, and willed her not to move, not to look away.

"Your mother told me it was time to get her," Gary said. His hands, Kate noticed, were behind his backside, one set casually over the other. The hands that had squeezed and fluttered and pushed. So indifferent, now. He frowned in Kate's direction, made a show of straightening his shirt again, and then moved quickly past Liz and down the stairs.

"Kate," Liz said. "What…" She gave her head a small, puzzled shake. "I think I'll be sick." She turned and pulled the door closed behind her, so quietly Kate strained to hear the catch. Kate would rather have heard a slam. A loud bang to shake away the numbness she suddenly felt. She heard Liz's steps on the stairs and then the sound she loved—Haley's bare feet flip-flopping across the kitchen floor. The flip-flopping stopped when Liz announced that the egg hunt was off and they were leaving right after breakfast.

Kate stared at the clock on her office wall. Ten seconds passed in silence.

"Gary's here," Liz said, at last. "I need to go."

"Wait," Kate said. After all this time, she couldn't let Liz go just like that. She had to say something. "Wait." She stared at her open office door and prayed no one would walk past. "I need to tell you—"

"This isn't about you," Liz cut in. She started to say something and then stopped. Kate heard Gary's voice in the distance, calling Liz's name.

"I didn't do anything," Kate said.

This time the silence was so long and so still Kate was not sure Liz was still there. Finally, Liz said flatly: "I know."

After Liz hung up, Kate sat with the phone against her ear. The dull buzz was strangely comforting. Even after she put the phone down, the drone went on and on in her mind, like the long stretches of highway that spread before her when she hopped on her bike for a long, long ride.

☙ ACKNOWLEDGEMENTS

As a short story writer, I am particularly grateful to the editors and others who keep all the "little magazines" going. Thank you to the editors of the following, where earlier versions of several of these stories were first published or broadcast: *The Journey Prize Stories 24*, *Meltwater: Fiction and Poetry from The Banff Centre for the Arts*, *Alberta Views*, *The Antigonish Review*, *Prairie Fire*, and CBC Radio's *Alberta Anthology*.

Most of these stories were started at Strawberry Creek Lodge. A huge thank you to Tena Wiebe and Brenda Kshyk for years and years of good food and for the special writing place, my writing "home-away-from-home." Thank you to the Writers' Guild of Alberta for arranging retreats at Strawberry Creek Lodge and to the Alberta Foundation for the Arts and the Banff Centre for funding and support for the writing of this collection.

The stories have taken a long and not-so-straight path and have been helped on the way by many people. Thank you to Kristjana Gunnars and Dave Margoshes for encouraging me, some time ago, to keep going. I am grateful to Caroline Adderson for getting to know the stories so well and for her frankness and encouragement. Heartfelt thanks to Betty Jane Hegerat, Tatiana Peet, Julie Robinson, Audrey Whitson, and Christine Wiesenthal for your critical eyes, thoughtful comments, and unwavering support. Thank you to my dad for lending your eyes after everybody else had a go. And to Peter Midgley, Cathie Crooks, and Monika Igali at the University of Alberta Press, thank you for your enthusiasm for the stories and for making a book.

Thank you, especially, to Herb for always ensuring that I have a Womanspace (aka my writing room). And to Bronwen and Charlotte, who added a few wiggles to the path: thank you for being.

Other Titles from
The University of Alberta Press

RUDY WIEBE: COLLECTED STORIES,
1955–2010

Rudy Wiebe
Thomas Wharton, Introduction

552 pages | Critical introduction, appendices, selected
bibliography
A volume in cuRRents, a Canadian Literature Series
978-0-88864-540-1 | $39.95 (T) paper
Literature/Short Stories

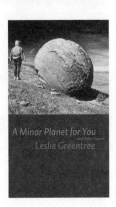

A MINOR PLANET FOR YOU
AND OTHER STORIES

Leslie Greentree

208 pages
A volume in cuRRents, a Canadian Literature Series
978-0-88864-465-7 | $24.95 (T) paper
Literature//Short Stories

RECURRING FICTIONS

Wendy McGrath

164 pages
A volume in cuRRents, a Canadian Literature Series
978-0-88864-389-6 | $16.95 (T) paper
Literature